'The mean streets of South London need their heroes tough. Private eye Nick Sharman fits the bill'
– *Telegraph*

'Full of cars, girls, guns, strung out along the high sierras of Brixton and Battersea, the Elephant and the North Peckham Estate, all those jewels in the crown they call Sarf London'
– *Arena*

mark timlin

gun street girl

The Third Nick Sharman Thriller

NO EXIT PRESS

This edition published in 2014
by No Exit Press
P.O.Box 394, Harpenden,
Herts, AL5 1XJ, UK

noexit.co.uk
@noexitpress

First published in 1990 by HEADLINE BOOK PUBLISHING PLC

A CIP catalogue record for this book is available from the British Library.

ISBN
978-1-84344-176-2 (print)
978-1-84344-177-9 (epub)
978-1-84344-178-6 (kindle)
978-1-84344-179-3 (pdf)

Typeset by Avocet Typeset, Somerton, Somerset
in 11 on 13.6pt Garamond
Printed in Great Britain by Clays Ltd, St Ives plc

For more information about Crime Fiction go to @CrimeTimeUK

4JP

1

It's funny how things start isn't it? I wanted a new necktie – no ordinary tie, mind. I fancied a real silk job that looked like it came from a minor public school or an offshoot from the Tory Party. Something impressive that would turn heads.

I was up in front of a jury, see. Nothing serious as it turned out. Nothing that a good brief and a lot of dough couldn't sort out. In fact, the morning I went out to buy the tie, I heard that the prosecution was shedding charges like cat's hair in the springtime. It was all boiling down to illegal helicopter parking and trespassing on international flying space. The Civil Aviation Authority wouldn't budge on that one.

So I went shopping for a tie in Bond Street and that's when I first saw her. I didn't know her name then, but I knew her game right off. She was doing a bit of up-market hoisting down South Molton Street. Now, I don't mind hoisters, never have, they don't do much harm – the losses go on the prices at the till. But most nicking from shops is done by the staff and that's a fact, and as a rule most hoisters don't get fisty when they're captured. They recognise it as part of the game and go quietly if they can't get away. Cut and run is their motto, or stand still for the nick. Not that there aren't one or two with a Stanley knife up their sleeves, but then crossing the road is dangerous, or so they tell me. In fact some of my best friends do a bit, and I don't mind admitting I've had the odd Blazer suit from a geezer in my local in my time.

I clocked her style after a couple of minutes. She was good, but not that good and I saw her stuffing a cashmere sweater into her tote bag in Brown's. I just saw the sleeve doing a David Nixon before she flipped the top shut. It's always strange to see someone on the hoist; it gave me a funny feeling, just like in the old days. You think: Gotcha! But you've got to pretend not to notice. That's how it was, anyway; now I don't care.

But old habits die hard and when she left Brown's I sauntered out after her, just to see if any of the staff had seen what I'd seen and were going to do the old 'Excuse me, madam, would you accompany me to the manager's office' bit. But she was off free and clear with no shop assistant following. She went across the street and into D-Mob. Not a good idea. They had security cameras fitted in there. I knew that for a fact; she obviously didn't.

I followed her into the shop and started going through a rack of jackets. She swanned around the floor, ran her hand along a shelf and palmed a pair of cufflinks and slid them into her coat pocket. Then she went over to the leathers and I had a chance to study her closely. She was about twenty-five or -six and darkly beautiful with thick auburn hair and perfectly made-up white skin. She was wearing sunglasses and a long red coat with huge sleeves and big pockets, and carried a giant leather bag. All the better to stash the loot, Granma. She stood about five nine in her heels and looked as if she was worth a packet. It's funny, but my mother always warned me about girls like that. West End girls she called them, and this one was about as West End as you could get. It was good camouflage but she was about to come unstuck. So I walked over to her and said, 'I'd put them back if I were you, love.'

'I'm not you, or your love, and I don't know what you're talking about,' she said.

'The two hundred nicker links in your pocket.'

'If you don't leave me alone I'll get the manager to call a policeman,' she said.

'Go ahead. The jumper in your bag isn't paid for either.'

'Are you the store detective?'

'No, but there's a spy in the sky here.'

'I beg your pardon?'

'Don't look now, but above the changing room door there's a little black circle. It's a camera lens.'

She couldn't resist and looked up, and frowned.

'Smile,' I said. 'You're on candid camera.'

'And who are you?'

'Well, right now whoever is looking at the screen figures I'm either your accomplice or I'm trying to chat you up.'

She was very cool, I'll give her that. 'And are you?' she asked. 'Trying to chat me up?'

I smiled. 'No, I don't think so. Maybe another time. But I am a detective, private.' I reached into my pocket, gave her my card. 'I don't care what you do but I used to be on the force and I do know that the people who own this shop always prosecute. From the look of you, you don't want that sort of publicity, so I'd put the cufflinks back or pay for them, okay?' She didn't say anything in reply so I simply added, 'Have a nice day.' And I left her and walked out of the shop.

In the street a big, handsome gorilla in chauffeur's livery loaded down with parcels and plastic bags clocked me straight off. He caught my eye and held it. I nodded and brushed past. No one came after me so they must have thought I was only chatting her up after all. Perhaps I was. I never got the tie but I did get off at the Bailey a week later and went back to work.

2

Two months went past before I spoke to her again. It was the third morning of what was to become the hottest summer since records began. Business was not good and I was sitting on a ticky tacky swivel chair behind a scarred desk in a steamy room in a town that was slowly dissolving like a grease spot on a hot stove. I sat and massaged my bad foot with my bad hand and listened out for trouble with my good ear.

I was alone in my office except for a little black and white neutered tom cat called Cat in memory of his mother. He was fast asleep with his head nearly in a saucer of water I'd put down for him less than an hour previously and which was already coated with a film of dust and contained the remains of a suicidal blue bottle.

I sighed, got up, changed the water, disturbed the cat, who meowed then went back to sleep again. I fell back into my seat and lit a Silk Cut king size and I saw the car draw up outside. It was a black Rolls-Royce limousine, 1989 model, stretched, but not indecently so. You couldn't have fitted a swimming pool into the back but there was probably room for a reasonable-sized jacuzzi. I watched it glide past my office window and I thought it was going to go on for ever. The black mirrored windows were closed tightly and I imagined the interior cool and dark from the air-conditioning. I levered myself up from the comfort of my chair and went and checked it out. The first thing that struck me about the car was that it was so clean. On that dusty morning the cellulose shone like a new razor blade. The second thing that struck me was the number plate. RP2, it read, which led me to believe that whoever owned the machine had a better one at home. It was an interesting thought.

The arrival of the limo even brought the local lads out of the pub on the corner for a squint and when they saw who disembarked they stayed for another and another.

The driver's door swung open smartly and a chauffeur in full black livery, including peaked cap and gaiters, hopped out and ran round to the passenger side. He was big and young and too handsome for his own good or my liking, with dark curls fighting to escape the restriction of his hat. His face was familiar, but I couldn't place it right away. I could remember the days when I had his energy, when I could hop because I wanted to rather than because I had to, and I kicked my bad foot against the door frame just to let it know I hadn't forgotten.

He gave the chaps gathered by the pub door a disdainful glance and flung the rear door open. He stood to attention, then extended his right hand to help his passenger alight. Out of the back of the vast, shining car stepped the hoister from South Molton Street and I suddenly remembered where I'd seen the chauffeur before.

That day she was dressed in black from head to toe, and her hair was bound tightly in a severe bunch at the back of her neck, pulled so tight that she almost seemed to be punishing the skin on her face. And the face itself, beautiful, but different under the same pair of shades she'd worn before. She stood for one moment with her hand on the driver's arm and whispered something to him. Then she made straight for my door.

I watched her take the few steps from the car to my office and the temperature in the room went up another few degrees. I opened the door for her and stepped back as she crossed the threshold. 'Hello again,' she said. 'I need your help.'

3

'Hello again yourself.' I directed her to the hard wooden chair on the window side of my desk. I went round to my own chair, sat down, pulled a foolscap pad in front of me and fumbled a pen out of the top drawer. In the short silence that followed I gave her the once-over.

Like I said, she was dressed all in black, from the tiny pillbox hat with a short veil that perched on the pulled-back hair, down to the wickedly pointed stiletto-heeled shoes she wore on her narrow feet. It was expensive black. Even without the car she'd arrived in I would have seen that. In spite of the unaccustomed heat she was wearing a suit — a costume, my Auntie Roz, who is eighty if she's a day, would have called it. Costume was a good description. It was cut tight to emphasise her figure. The jacket was short, bolero length, and double-breasted over a pencil-slim skirt that reached just below her knees and had a long split up the back seam. Under the jacket was a black silk blouse buttoned severely to the neck. She wore black stockings on her long, slender legs. Over her shoulder she carried a big, fat, soft leather handbag that screamed Gucci. She wore no jewellery.

Finally she broke the silence. 'What's the matter, cat got your tongue?'

'No,' I said. 'Now let me guess. You've been nicked and you've come to me for a character reference?'

'Not very funny, Mr Sharman.'

'It wasn't meant to be funny. What is all this?'

She took off her sunglasses. Her eyes were the most exquisite shade of blue I'd ever seen, the colour of Forget-Me-Nots. And beautiful, even enamelled with grief as they were. Free of make-up and full of tears and slightly puffed. If anything, the naked sadness in her eyes made her more attractive. The cool rich exterior and the terrible sadness within. She was in mourning and on her it looked good. She crossed her legs and the sound of silk on silk was like bated breath. 'You're staring, Mr Sharman.' Her voice was barely a sigh.

'It's not every day a beautiful woman comes to see me. I wonder if you'd mind elaborating.'

'Of course,' she replied, and hesitated.

'Yes?' I prompted.

'You don't know who I am, do you?'

'No.'

'My name is Pike.' She put her sunglasses on my desk. 'Elizabeth Pike. My father was Robert Pike.' She started to cry. She opened her handbag and felt around in it until she found a black-edged handkerchief which she pressed to her already bruised eyes.

'Of course,' I said. 'RP2, Sir Robert Pike.'

'You know then,' she said between sobs.

'I know that he's dead.' Her sobs got deeper. 'I'm sorry.' I stood up and went and perched on the edge of the desk in front of her. 'Do you fancy a drink of anything?' I asked. I knew I did.

'No, thank you.'

I offered her a cigarette from my packet and she accepted. As I lit first hers and then another for myself, I ran what I knew about

Robert Pike through my mind. It was quite a lot. He had been that sort of man.

Sir Robert was an entrepreneur, the millionaire owner of a vast publishing empire. He started off delivering newspapers in the thirties and ended up owning them in the eighties. Newspapers and magazines, followed by TV stations, a football team, record companies and other media and leisure-orientated businesses, with branches in property, transport and so much else it would make your head spin. He was rich, stinking rich, and seemed to enjoy it.

He was a man who spent the money he earned. He was a great collector. He bought paintings by old masters and new talent alike. He had a huge library of first editions, from Charles Dickens to twentieth-century writers like Mailer and Ian Fleming. He was also reputed to have one of the most valuable collections of American comic books in the world. Plus he amassed houses in all sorts of exotic locations, where he entertained other rich and famous men. But his favourite hobby, above all others, was collecting rare cars. He had more concourse-condition automobiles than you could decently shake a stick at.

He had managed to amass his great fortune and still remain virtually unknown to the public. He did not like publicity, even though in the scheme of things publicity liked him. The one and only scandalous part of his past, the sudden appearance of a previously unknown illegitimate child who had lived all of her life in Australia, had the great man's lawyers papering the walls with enough writs to keep the courts busy for years. The story vanished from his rivals' headlines almost as quickly as it had appeared.

So when Robert Pike took his old Webley service revolver and stuck it in his mouth and pulled the trigger a couple of weeks previously, you would have been hard pressed to miss the story. The verdict had been suicide. Pretty reasonable under the circumstances, I would have thought. This time the story had been plastered all over the press with no danger of litigation. His own papers canonised his memory; the papers that belonged to the other press lords dug the dirt.

Then it suddenly came to me where else I had seen Elizabeth Pike. Sir Robert's funeral had been big TV news just a few days ago. Looking at her now, in front of me, holding her tear-stained handkerchief, I remembered seeing her then, being supported by a male relative as she entered Westminster Cathedral for the memorial service, but it hadn't clicked. I also remembered a stunning blonde at the ceremony, described as Sir Robert's other daughter.

'I saw you on TV,' I said. 'At the funeral.'

'Congratulations.'

I felt as if I was going down the wrong road. What the hell do you say? Did you enjoy the service? Did they serve ham or tongue in the bridge rolls at the do afterwards? 'I didn't recognise you,' was all I said.

'No, I didn't pinch the altar piece.' Her tone was dry. She dragged the smoke from the cigarette deep into her lungs and expelled it in one long, blue plume.

'Miss Pike,' I said, 'if you need my help, I'll do what I can.'

She nodded.

'So tell me about it.'

'Where do I start?' she asked.

'The beginning is usually good.'

'The beginning,' she repeated, like a child, as I went back to my chair. 'Yes, that is a good place.'

And so she started. 'It began a long time ago, before I was born, actually. My father had an affair with one of the women who worked for him. Her name was Joanna Bennett, with two 't's. She became pregnant at about the same time as my mother was pregnant with me.'

Inconvenient, I thought.

'My father offered to pay for Joanna to have an abortion,' Elizabeth Pike continued. 'She refused. She insisted that she loved him. He couldn't bear the thought of any scandal besmirching the family name. He thought it would kill my mother. It probably would have. My father was a very honourable man, or so he thought.' Her face twisted slightly at that. 'His idea of honour was to push the poor woman off to Australia. I tend to think he was just an uptight bastard who couldn't bear to have his good name dragged through the divorce courts. That would really have besmirched it. Times were different then, even if they did call them the swinging sixties.'

'You didn't like your father?'

'I didn't say that, but you're right, I didn't much. But he changed after my mother died and I did get to like him, and now I miss him. Maybe it really was her he was trying to protect all along.'

'When did she die?' I asked.

'Five years ago. In Australia, of all places. She was on holiday and drowned in an accident on the Great Barrier Reef. She'd always wanted to see it, but Daddy just refused to set foot over there. We always said it was because of Murdoch. We know better now.'

'We?'

'My brother and I, Mother too, but of course she's not here now to know anything.' She paused sadly. 'Anyway, where was I?'

'Your mother died in Australia.'

'Yes, that's right.'

'And?'

'And my father changed. He told us about our half-sister Catherine. It was a hell of a shock. She's the same age as me, and I had no idea she even existed. Then I met her.'

'How old were you then?'

'When I met her? Twenty-one.'

'And she was in this country?'

'Yes, she just arrived one day not long after my mother's death. She had no relatives in Australia, no one close at all. Apparently she and Joanna had lived like gypsies, moving from place to place since she was born. They always lived in hotels. My father made Joanna an allowance, a generous one at that, but she's never got over being banished. That was one of the conditions my father made, you see. She must live in Australia and never ever return. Apparently she loathed the place. She was an English rose who just dried up in the heat, and she took to drink.'

'To keep her moist,' I said.

Elizabeth Pike looked at me from under thick, dark eyelashes. 'You're a cynic, Mr Sharman. I expected as much.'

'I'm glad I didn't disappoint you. What were the other conditions?'

'There were two more. The fact of the child must never be made public, and Joanna was never to get in touch with my father again, or else the deal was off.'

'But he made it public himself, if I remember rightly.'

'He allowed it to be made public,' she corrected me. 'He said he wanted to stop living a lie. But as I said, he'd changed, mellowed, and by then both the women were dead of course.'

'Of course,' I said. 'Go on with the story.'

She collected her thoughts. 'Yes, Joanna died in 1982 and Catherine disappeared for a time. There was some trouble with drugs, she went off the rails. She was desperately lonely and scared. Daddy kept paying the allowance into Joanna's bank, for Catherine, you understand. He arranged it so that she could draw the money, but it wasn't touched for ages. And then she turned up out of the blue, one day in London.'

'Quite a surprise.'

'It was, Daddy nearly threw a fit. He'd never even seen her. Thank goodness she was discreet, and clever too. It was a hell of a job to get to him. All sorts of crazy people try. When you're as rich and powerful as he was, everyone wants a bit of you, a bit of your time. I think that people thought something would rub off, some bit of his magic.'

'Or some bit of his cash,' I said. 'Sorry, I'm being cynical again.'

'I'm getting used to it. Apparently she got friendly with one of Daddy's secretaries, found out where he'd be one evening and turned up.'

'Didn't her mother have a contact number or address?'

'Oh no. No contact under any circumstances.'

'So what happened then?'

'Daddy fell for Catherine, literally. He helped her financially – she wanted to be an actress – and bought her a house, although in the end she virtually moved in with us.'

'Very generous,' I said. 'But you told me he'd never seen her. What proof did she have that she was who she said she was?'

'Everything. It's all still at the house in Daddy's safe. Birth certificate, medical and school records, although she didn't go to school much from what we can gather – she got her education the hard way – her mother's death certificate and the record of all the payments Father made to her. She also had a scrapbook of anything she had ever found about Robert Pike. That really did it for Daddy. The fact that although he ignored her, she thought enough about him to collect stories about him. Anyway, no one knew about her but Daddy. She could hardly invent herself.'

'So she could have blown the gaff on the old man at any time?'

Elizabeth Pike's eyes flashed with anger. 'Please don't call him that.'

'I'm sorry,' I said, and I was. 'But she could have.'

'She didn't need to. He wanted to help her. He felt guilty about neglecting her and, besides, she's charming as well as gorgeous. You'll see.'

'I already have,' I said.

'What?'

'Seen her.'

'Where?'

'On TV.'

'Of course.'

'So what's the problem?'

'There are a couple,' said Elizabeth Pike. 'Since my father died, Catherine has changed.'

'How?'

'I don't know exactly, but I think she's scared.'

'Of what?'

'I don't know, she won't say.'

'You said "a couple".'

'I was coming to that. I've been through my father's records with the accountants. His personal financial records. He was paying Joanna Bennett out of his private bank account, you see, to keep the payments secret. He was paying someone else in Australia too.'

'Who?'

'Someone called Joseph Lorimar.'

'Why?'

'I don't know.'

'What sort of payments?'

'Regular large payments, larger than he made to Joanna.'

'How much and for how long?'

'They started in 1970. At the time, it was ten thousand a month.'

I whistled. 'That was a lot then.'

'It was, and they increased. The last payment was for fifty thousand pounds.'

'When was that?'

'The same month that my mother died.'

'And then?'

'Nothing.'

'How was the money paid?'

'By banker's draft to the National Bank of Perth. I had some enquiries made. Apparently Lorimar opened the account with a small deposit. The money that my father paid in was withdrawn from various branches of the bank in cash. Not in large enough amounts to cause a stir. No one remembers Lorimar. The official who opened the account is dead. The account is still open but hasn't been used since the last withdrawal.'

'So who is Lorimar?'

'As far as I can ascertain, he doesn't exist. I'm sure there are people by that name in Australia, but I can't find any trace of the man who opened that bank account.'

'And the last payment coincided with the death of your mother?'

She nodded.

'Just as a matter of interest, where was Catherine when that happened?'

She looked at me and her eyes widened. 'You can't think ... It was an accident. My mother went out on a charter boat. It hit a submerged wreck. Everyone on board died. You can't think that Catherine had anything to do with it. That's ridiculous.'

'It was only a thought, Miss Pike,' I said.

'You have a suspicious mind, Mr Sharman.'

'I am paid to have a suspicious mind. And my suspicious mind asks me why you care so much about your half-sister.'

'What do you mean?'

'Exactly what I say,' I said.

'You don't know her. I care as much about her as anyone else in the world. She is part of my family, and my family is the most important thing to me.'

The room went silent except for the sound of cars rushing down the main road.

'So what do you want me to do?' I asked.

'I want you to protect Catherine and try to discover what's bothering her. To try and find out why my father died. To dig around for anything that will explain what happened. I want the truth.'

'The truth sometimes hurts.' I knew that for a fact.

'The truth can also set you free,' she said. There was no arguing with that. 'And now we've got the clichés out of the way, can we get back to business? My father died under mysterious circumstances and no one is prepared to do anything about it.'

'I'd hardly say mysterious. Unusual maybe, tragic certainly. If I remember rightly the coroner's verdict was suicide.'

She looked as if she was going to spit in my eye. 'You read the papers.'

'I could hardly have missed it. I read one owned by your father.'

'Late father.'

'Sorry.'

'Which one?' she asked.

'The one with the long words and no half-naked women on page three.'

'A snob, Mr Sharman. It hardly goes with the surroundings.'

I looked around my shabby office and then back at her. Her grooming, even in mourning, made the place, and me, for that matter, look even more shabby. 'Not all of us,' I said, 'were fortunate enough to be born with money and privilege and still do a bit of hoisting on the side.'

'Rude too,' she added. 'I'm glad you can afford to be so cavalier with prospective clients.'

'I can't, but I am,' I said. 'I choose my clients with care.' Which I patently don't.

'A rugged individualist.'

'So I've been told.'

'That's exactly what I need.'

'Why not use your own people? I imagine a company as big as Pike has its own security force or can tap into one of the big boys for help. And anyway, surely Australia is the place to start.'

'I've got nothing to go on but intuition. The authorities are convinced that Daddy killed himself. And the Australian end dried up with the last payment to Lorimar. I used our people to get the information I've given you. Banks don't give that sort of information readily. And you're wrong, Mr Sharman, anything that's happening is happening here, in London.'

'So get your people here on the job.'

'I don't trust them to do it properly.'

'But you trust me?'

'You saw me shoplifting and didn't turn me in, you helped me.'

'That's hardly a recommendation.'

'And I read about your trial in the papers.'

'Nor is that.'

'I don't know. You came out of it all right. You're honourable, and you're not bribable.'

'Everyone is, you've just got to find the right bribe,' I said.

'And you finish the job,' she went on as if I hadn't spoken.

'There is that, I suppose,' I agreed drily.

'Well?'

'Go to the police.'

'The police wouldn't be interested. They'd simply go along with what the coroner said.'

'That's fair enough,' I replied. 'I'd expect that they would. But you say differently.'

'I know differently.'

'How?'

'I just do,' she said stubbornly, and I supposed that in her world, when she said something it became true. I felt like telling her to join the rest of us in the real world. But like she said, she was a prospective client and she had money, so I let it ride. Like a jockey.

'Your father was rich,' I said.

'An understatement,' she replied.

'Who inherits?' I asked.

'Who knows?'

'You mean you don't?'

'My father was very good at keeping secrets. He kept a daughter hidden for over twenty years. He wasn't an old man and his will was his own affair. Pike Publications will always remain in the family, that I know for certain. Other than that only my father and his solicitor knew. The reading is the day after tomorrow.'

'Why so long after the funeral?' I asked.

'David had to fly to the States immediately and it couldn't be read without his presence.'

'Breaths are bated,' I said.

'You could say that,' she replied with the certainty of someone who would never be short of money.

'Did he leave a note?' I asked. 'I can't remember one being mentioned.'

She shook her head. 'No, no note.'

'That *is* strange, most suicides like to leave a last few words. But then I suppose he lived by words. Maybe he was right out of them.'

'I can think of no reason why he might kill himself.'

'You'd be surprised by the reasons that finally make people do it. The last straw can be a very tiny thing.'

She looked over at me and started to cry again, and I realised I was stamping all over her life in my size tens. I went round the desk and squatted awkwardly by her and took her hand. It was a lovely hand, I noticed, with only a single chewed thumbnail to mar it. I could have held it for a very long time. She was trembling and I squeezed her beautiful fingers. 'I'm sorry if talking about it is making it worse. I'll do what I can to help, but there's a lot more I'll have to know. Can I get you something?'

'Another cigarette and perhaps some coffee.'

I stood up and handed her another Silk Cut. I prepared two mugs of instant in my little back room. When I took the coffee through she had stopped crying. I lit myself a cigarette too and sipped at my drink. It was disgusting. I could see that she agreed but was too polite to mention it. I liked her for that. Then the cat woke up and jumped onto her lap. I told her to shove him off but she wouldn't, even when he dug his claws into her expensive skirt and, from the look on her face, the expensive legs beneath. I liked her for that too.

'By the way. How do you know about all this?' I asked after a moment.

'What?'

'All the details about Catherine and her mother.'

'From my father. In the end he didn't mind talking about it. I think he found it was a relief in a way. And from Catherine herself. We've become great friends, although she doesn't like talking about her early life much. It was tough.'

'But your father never mentioned the other payments. The Lorimar payments?'

'No, they only showed up since he died.'

'Who found your father?' I asked. I hoped that it hadn't been her.

'Our butler, Courtneidge,' she said without self-consciousness, as if everyone had a butler.

'Forgive me, but I forget, where was this?'

'In his study.'

'No, where's the house?'

'Our town house, in Curzon Street.'

'Who else was in the house at the time?'

'Our two maids, Miranda and Constance, and Cook. Everyone else was out.'

'Who is everyone else and where were they? I'm just interested,' I added quickly to forestall any more comments about my suspicious mind.

She thought for a moment. 'Catherine was at the theatre with Simon. He's our cousin. He's a house guest at the moment. Vincent – that's our chauffeur – drove them. I was at dinner with a friend.' She reddened slightly and I felt a twinge of jealousy for the lucky man. 'And David, that's my brother, was at a publishing function with his wife Claire.'

'How long have your servants been with you?'

'Courtneidge for ever. He joined Daddy just after the war when he started to make money. Cook came to us ten years ago at least.

Miranda and Constance have been with us for a couple of years and Vincent started driving Daddy just a few months ago when his other driver left.'

'I see, everyone accounted for. That's good.'

'Do you think that Daddy might have been murdered?'

'I don't think anything, yet, but you seem to.'

'I don't know what to think. My head aches when I do think about it. I want you to look into it. Will you take the job, please?'

How could I refuse? 'You're convinced something is going on, aren't you?' I asked.

She nodded.

'All right,' I said. 'I'll see what I can do. No promises, you understand. You might be all wrong about this. When would you want me to start?'

'I want you to start right now, today. And I want you on hand twenty-four hours a day. You can stay at the house. There's plenty of room. You'll be comfortable, I guarantee.' She went from pleading to bossing in the wink of an eye. Rich people, see.

'No so fast,' I interrupted. 'I can't just drop everything. I have arrangements to make.'

'What kind of arrangements?' she asked, as if I was just sitting around with nothing to do but jump at her command. Which I was in a way, but she didn't have to know that.

I nodded towards my cat who was lying comatose on her lap. 'That kind of arrangement, for one thing. I can't just dump the poor little bugger on the street. I have a friend who'll take care of him. Why don't I sort myself out and meet you tomorrow?'

'Because there's an important reception we have to attend tonight. I want you there to nose around for information.'

'Reception?' I asked, smelling a free drink or ten.

'Yes, we're going to the launch of our new magazine. It's called *Cause Célèbre*, a sort of glossy mix of *Interview* and *Ritz*.'

I was glad that I was hip and knew what she was talking about.

'It's rubbish really,' she went on. 'But it was my father's last project. He thought it would sell and who am I to argue?'

Who indeed? I thought.

'The reception is at the Crypt Club in Dean Street, beginning at ten. You'll have a chance to meet a lot of the people involved with Pike's.'

I can hardly wait, I thought.

'And then tomorrow you can meet David.'

'Won't David be at the reception?'

'No, he won't be back from the States until tomorrow.'

'Just out of interest, how did your brother take to having Catherine turn up. Like a sort of cuckoo in the nest.'

'He wasn't keen at first, but he came round. He's not crazy about women.' I looked at her, and she blushed. 'No, I don't mean that. He's married, after all. It's just that he's a man's man. Daddy wanted that. And especially where the business is involved. David thinks it's a sort of exclusive gentlemen's club. I'm hosting the party tonight and he thinks it will be a disaster. Catherine will be there, you can keep her company.'

'Okay,' I said. 'Just give me some details and I'll catch up with you this evening.'

'Such as?' she queried.

'If I'm coming to stay, I should know what number Curzon Street you live.'

She told me.

'Telephone number?'

She gave me a number which I jotted down on the pad under the notes I had made. I looked at my watch and was glad I hadn't had to hock the Rolex. 'It's nearly one now,' I said. 'I should be with you by five, six at the latest.'

'Excellent. You can join Catherine for dinner. I have things to do, so I'll leave you to get acquainted. And would you mind wearing a jacket?'

'Tails?' I asked.

'A lounge suit will be sufficient, and a tie, if you don't mind.'

It was funny that she mentioned a tie. 'I believe I can still remember how to knot one.'

'Good. Now, one last thing, your fee.'

I thought she was never going to mention it.

'I believe you charge two hundred pounds a day,' she said, all business.

'You've been checking up on me.'

'Of course. That is your fee, isn't it?'

'Plus expenses and mileage.'

'There should be no expenses, and you won't need a car, you'll travel with us in the Rolls. However, if you do incur any out of pocket expenses, you must obtain receipts and submit them on a company expense sheet that I will provide. You can pay them out of your advance.'

'Advance?'

She bent down to dig into her huge handbag yet again and disturbed the cat. He jumped down and gave her a dirty look and went back to his favourite spot by his drinking bowl. Out of the bag she pulled two banded bricks of bank notes. 'Ten days in advance,' she said. 'Two thousand pounds. If you supply me with a VAT invoice I will see that the amount is made up.'

'I'm not registered.'

She nodded as if to say that she guessed as much. 'I'd appreciate a receipt anyway.'

If she thought I was going to offer a discount for cash, no questions asked, she was barking up the wrong alley. Although it was a tempting idea, my bank account being in the state it was. But I wouldn't give her the satisfaction. 'I'll let you have one,' I said.

'Thank you.'

'What are the rest of the family going to say about me moving in?' I asked. 'Do they know you're here?'

'I may invite whom I like to the house for whatever reason I choose. The money I just paid you is mine, and it's my business what I do with it.'

'So they're probably going to hate me.'

'Probably.' She stood up.

'This evening then,' I said, following her to the door.

'I'll look forward to it. I'll have something cool waiting for you.'

By the way her attitude had changed, and from what she'd just told me, I suspected it might be my welcome, but I let it go.

4

I escorted Elizabeth Pike to her car. The weather man on the news that morning had forecast temperatures in the low eighties and the sun burnt down from a clear sky. My new client seemed cool enough however, especially for someone with sudden death on her mind.

As we left the office, the chauffeur bounded from his seat, but I was too quick for him. I opened the Rolls's passenger door and got hit with a blast of frigid, perfumed air from inside the car. 'That's all right, Vincent. I can manage,' I said and he gave me a dirty look as he stood and watched me help his mistress into her seat. I wasn't surprised he was miffed as I caught a flash of white thigh as she settled herself into the leather upholstery. It was obviously a perk of the job. One of the lads standing outside the pub door with a pint of chemical lager in his hand gave him a wolf whistle and Vincent reddened. I gave him a wink which didn't help. He scowled under his uniform cap and went back to his steering wheel. I leant down and said to Elizabeth Pike, 'Moody, isn't he?'

'Don't tease him,' she said. 'He's been very good to us.'

I bet, I thought, but merely said 'I'll see you later.' And closed the door.

The car started with barely a rumble and Vincent executed a tight three-point turn before joining the town-bound traffic flow on the main road. I watched the huge car disappear into the one-way system like a big black beetle surrounded by a horde of lesser bugs of various colours and went back into my office.

I checked my address book and got straight on the phone to Wanda, the cat woman. She answered on the fifteenth ring, when I'd almost given up on her. I identified myself and she gave me a bollocking for not having been in touch for so long.

'Sorry, Wanda,' I said. 'I haven't had much of a social life lately.' Then she went all mumsy on me, but I soon knocked that on the head. 'Listen, I need a favour,' I interrupted.

'That's the only time you ever do get in touch,' she wailed, and it was true.

I apologised again and eventually she came round because she's good that way, and I realised how much she meant to me and how much I'd neglected her. I explained that I had to go away for a while and of course she agreed to take care of Cat. As she had about fifty other moggies around the house I guessed that one more or less wouldn't make much difference. Besides, they were old friends. She'd looked after him before. I told her that we'd be with her in fifteen minutes and hung up the receiver.

I picked up Cat and slung him round my neck where he likes to sit as a sort of treat from time to time, even though it was rather warm for a fur collar, took my notebook and got on my way. I locked up my office and walked up to where my E-Type was parked. I peeled the cat off my shoulders and put him on the passenger seat. He gave me a growl and turned his back, just like his mum would have done. I dropped the notebook next to him and started the car. Once we'd got going he stood up with his front paws on the passenger door handle and clocked the scenery through the window.

We doodled through to Brixton and I ducked into the back doubles to where Wanda was now the proud owner of a very des-res. Three years ago you could have flogged the whole terrace of three houses for a hundred thousand quid. Then came the property boom and the going rate went through the ceiling. Then came the slump and who the hell knows what next.

I hammered on the door and waited. After a few minutes I hammered again and eventually I saw a shape behind the glass of the door and she opened it. She was dressed in a loose robe that left little to the imagination, and not much underneath. There seemed to be skin popping out everywhere I looked.

'Do yourself up, love,' I said. 'You'll frighten the animal.'

As it goes, though, Wanda's in pretty good shape for a woman her age. She's got a few years on me and I'm hoping I'm half as trim when I'm knocking on forty's door.

'Don't be so bloody cheeky, Nick. I've been out the back getting a tan.' She was a good colour but she still cherried up.

'Giving the neighbours a treat, are you?' I asked. 'Some of the old sods round here will have a coronary if they see you like that. I expect one or two have taken themselves in hand about it already?'

She blushed even more and drew the robe round herself. 'Are you coming in, or what?'

'I can't,' I said. 'I've got to get packed for this job.' I looked at my watch. 'And I think I've still got time for a little shopping before I go. Apparently I'm not quite sartorially correct for the company I'm going to keep.'

'Are you going to get into more trouble?' asked Wanda, and I think she really cared.

'No. I'm just going to be a rich woman's plaything for a bit. She thinks someone is up to some dirty work at the crossroads.'

'And is she right?'

I shrugged. 'Dunno. I doubt it, too much money, see. It breeds paranoia.'

'Well, be careful,' she warned. 'I know you. You can get into trouble anywhere.'

'The story of my life, Wanda.'

'How long will you be gone?'

'I don't know that either. As long as it takes, I suppose.'

'Well, give him to me,' she said, reaching out for Cat. 'And when you get back you can come and be my plaything for a bit.'

'It's a date,' I said.

As she took Cat from me, her robe opened and one firm breast popped into view.

'Don't move,' I said. 'I want to remember you just as you are.'

Now she was crimson from sun and embarrassment and I laughed like I hadn't laughed for months. Eventually she joined in and I realised how much I'd missed her. 'You're on for the best dinner of your life when I get back,' I told her.

'And afterwards?' she asked.

'Perhaps you'll have my body.'

'Promises, promises.'

'You'll have to join the queue, like everyone else.'

'And who else is in the queue?'

'Nobody at the moment,' I said. 'So don't go far.'

I leaned down and planted a kiss at the side of her mouth. She smelled all warm and clean and I didn't really want to go, but I had to. 'I'll see you soon, Wanda. Thanks for everything.'

I walked back down the short garden path and climbed into the Jaguar. When I looked back she was still standing in the doorway clutching Cat to her breast. I smiled and waved as I drove off and she smiled back.

By then it was almost two o'clock and I drove from Brixton to Bond Street, a journey that wasn't half as long as it used to be. I hid the car away on Woodstock Street and with one eye open for the clamp van I dived into a couple of shops to get some new threads. It's amazing what a couple of grand in cash can do for your self-confidence. I bought half a dozen shirts, a couple of ties, three, count 'em, three lightweight suits in dark colours from an

Italian designer who could retire on what they cost me, and a dozen pairs of cotton socks in various colours. I also picked up a new pair of tasselled loafers, and with a big hole in my advance I got back to the car just in time to be presented with a parking ticket in a nice little transparent bag.

'Cheers,' I said to the warden and tossed the ticket into the back with my shopping. First legitimate out of pocket expense, I thought.

It was getting late so I beat the rush back to Tulse Hill, had a shower, got dressed in a new yellow shirt and dark patterned tie. Slid into one of my new suits, a grey checked number that I thought went well with my complexion, navy socks and my new St Louis. I felt like the business.

I kept my new clobber in its fancy carrier bags then packed my battered old Samsonite with a couple of pairs of blue jeans, a light jacket, a pair of thick-soled brogues, as many pairs of boxer shorts as I could tuck round the edges, a wash bag complete with a new tube of toothpaste and the white towelling robe I'd nicked once when staying at the Albany in Glasgow. I remembered what Elizabeth Pike had said about driving and I called a cab to collect me at four. For once, Third World Cars were almost on time.

I turned off the gas and locked up my flat and staggered down to the car under the weight of my luggage with my old trusty trench coat over my shoulder even though it looked as if it was never going to rain again. The cabby watched me struggle with the door and eventually deigned to lean over and unlock it. When I was all settled and managed to get him to drop the decibel count of the Bob Marley tape to below the pain level, I was on my way back to the West End again.

Oh yeah, I forgot. As an accessory to my new whistle I was wearing a six-shot Browning Baby in an ankle holster, and just in case of emergencies I had tucked an S&W 357 Combat Magnum with Hogue rubber grips and a 2½-inch barrel in a greasy shoulder holster, plus a box of ammunition, between two pairs of Levis in my case.

I've learnt that you can't be too careful in this life.

5

Just after five o'clock in the evening the cabby drew up outside a beautiful four-storey Georgian terraced house in Curzon Street. I checked it through the nicotine-stained car window as I waited for my change from a tenner.

Very pleasant, all mod cons, handy for the shops and not much change out of three million smackers, I guessed.

Now don't get me wrong, I'm not knocking property. My little attic in Norwood had nearly doubled in value in the eighteen months before the property crash. I just had a niggling worry that within a mile, maybe two, from where I was sitting there were cardboard cities underneath the arches at Charing Cross and Waterloo, and just possibly it was a tiny bit immoral for one family to own so much real estate when a brisk walk could take you to where there were a couple of hundred people living rough, who between them couldn't raise the cost of having this gaff's windows cleaned.

I shoved the thought to the back of my mind as I collected my cash, left the car and rescued my luggage from the boot. I climbed three stone steps, flanked by iron railings, and rang the door bell. After a few moments a pretty young girl in a black dress covered with a stiff white apron opened the door. I placed my case and bags between my feet and tried to look as if I belonged.

'Is Miss Pike at home?' I asked. 'Miss Elizabeth Pike.'

'Mr Sharman?'

'That's right.'

'You're expected, sir. I'll get Vincent to fetch your luggage.'

'No need,' I said. 'I've managed it so far.'

She gave me an old-fashioned look but allowed me to carry my stuff over the threshold.

'I'll show you to your room.'

'Thanks.' I smiled.

'This way.' She led me to a polished wooden lift shaft that ran up through the centre of the house.

'This is unusual,' I said for something to say.

'It's a bit old and slow, but it saves my feet, I can tell you.' She slid the latticed door open for me and we stood facing each other as the lift rose to the top floor.

'Are you Miranda or Constance?'

'Miranda,' she replied. 'How did you know?'

'It's my job, ma'am.'

She smiled, then got serious. 'Are you here to investigate us?'

'You know what I do then?'

She reddened, and I noticed a mist of perspiration on her top lip. She brushed at it with the back of her hand. 'I wasn't being nosy,' she assured me. 'It's just that you overhear things.'

'Don't worry, Miranda,' I said. 'I'm sure you do.'

'People forget we're around, you see, they treat us like pieces of furniture.'

'Does that upset you?'

'No, you get used to it.'

'So you like your job.'

'I've liked it better since Miss Catherine arrived. She's different to the others, much more fun, and we had parties, until … ' She didn't finish.

'I know,' I said as the lift clanged to a halt.

'Oh, please don't say I said that. It was a terrible shame, Sir Robert killing himself like that, but a private detective, that's so exciting.' She flushed. 'I read detective stories all the time. Ruth Rendell's my favourite – '

I cut her off. 'It's not like that in real life,' I said and changed the subject. 'You were here that night, weren't you?'

'Yes.'

'Then I would like to talk to you sometime when you have a moment.'

'Any time,' she said, and we stood awkwardly in the intimacy of the small wooden box.

She opened the door again for me and took me down a long corridor that smelled of Johnson's Wax and into a large, high-ceilinged sitting room. The room contained a Chesterfield sofa upholstered in flowered moquette and a matching armchair, a console-sized TV and a delicate, dark wood table upon which sat a vase of fresh flowers. One wall contained built-in bookshelves, stuffed with soft- and hard-covered books broken only by a closed door. There was another door, slightly ajar, in the wall opposite us.

'This is your suite, Mr Sharman.' Miranda walked across the soft carpet and pushed the door opposite wide. 'The bedroom is in here and the bathroom beyond.'

I followed her and peered over her shoulder. The bedroom was furnished with a double bed, a portable TV on a trolley at its foot, a wardrobe, a dressing table with mirror, and a chest of drawers. On top of the chest stood another vase of flowers. Next to the chest was a small refrigerator. Mayfair, all the comforts of home and all for nixes. Can't be bad, I thought. I pointed to the closed door. 'What's through there?'

'That door leads to Miss Catherine's private apartment. It's locked,' she added.

'I imagine it would be,' I said. 'Who has the key?'

'Courtneidge has one, Miss Catherine has the other.'

'Thank you,' I said. The windows in both rooms were open to allow whatever faint breeze there was to enter the room. The curtains hardly moved in the heat and I could smell the park, close and sour like an old lion sleeping in the sun.

'If it's too hot for you I'll shut the windows and turn on the air-conditioning,' said Miranda.

'No, leave it. It suits me fine.'

'Of course.' She smiled. 'Miss Elizabeth asked that you meet her in the conservatory at six for a drink before dinner. The party doesn't start until late so there's plenty of time.'

'That sounds good to me.'

'I'll leave you alone now.'

'All right,' I replied. 'I'll just freshen up and I'll be ready. Where is the conservatory, by the way?'

'On the ground floor at the back of the house. If you ring,' she showed me a brass bell push by the bed, 'I'll come and show you.'

'I don't want to be any trouble,' I said. 'I'm sure I'll find it.'

'No trouble,' she replied. 'But as you wish.'

She smiled again, turned on her heel with a flounce of petticoat and left the room, closing the door behind her and leaving just a faint trace of sweet-scented soap behind.

I put my case on the bed and opened it. I found my second gun and stashed it away on the top of the wardrobe, right at the back. It wouldn't last a minute if someone good spun the drum. But I hoped that anyone who searched the room would be an amateur. I switched on the TV set in the bedroom, looking for the news, but it was too early so I left the set tuned to a quiz show and went and fixed myself a drink from the fridge. It was well stocked with beer and mixes and hard liquor in miniature bottles. There was a bucket of ice and freshly cut lemon and lime slices in a dish. I made myself a vodka and tonic. Listening to the bubbles hissing to the top of the glass made me feel cooler. My shirt was soaked from the journey so I unwrapped a fresh one and hung it on the back of the bathroom door. I filled the sink with lukewarm water and washed. I cleaned my teeth and rinsed my mouth out with a fresh drink, then dirtied it again with a fresh cigarette.

The programme changed on the TV and I caught the beginning of the news as I put on a new pink shirt and re-knotted my tie. I put my jacket back on and took a gander in the wardrobe mirror. I didn't look half bad, I thought, or half good for that matter. I stood for a moment at the window in the shadow of the Hilton looking up through a metal fire escape at the anonymous windows of the hotel, then left the suite wondering what my first evening as a private detective in residence would bring.

I walked back down the corridor and decided to take the stairs to the ground floor. I looked down each hallway as I came to it and each was more ornate than the last.

When I got to the ground floor, I headed away from the front door towards the back of the house. The place was furnished like a palace. It was full of antique furniture and the pictures on the walls were by people whose signatures were worth millions. The floors were covered by carpets so old and fine that their patterns were all but faded into memory. I kept walking and eventually came to a set of double doors standing ajar. I could hear faint music and I pushed the lefthand door open and found Elizabeth Pike.

She was listening to Mahler playing on a radiogram that had been made when records were thick and breakable and twelve inches in diameter and the autochange had just been invented. There was a pile of them on top of the record player and their labels were printed with the names of record companies that had long ago vanished into history. The whole room was like something out of Raffles Hotel, Singapore, pre-war. Or at least what the movies would have us believe it was like. The furniture was made of cane and covered with jungle prints. There were indoor plants everywhere and a fan turned indolently to try and put some life into the heated air. There was a professional wet bar against one glass wall and the sun was caught among the bottles and glasses and winked at me suggestively. On top of the bar was a framed photograph of a man and a woman taken in the conservatory. The man I recognised as Sir Robert Pike. The woman was middle-aged with greying hair and startling blue eyes. I could see Elizabeth in twenty years' time in her features.

The conservatory ceiling was made of glass, but thankfully an awning had been drawn across to shield the inside from most of the rays. Even so it was very warm in there and smelled slightly of valves from the record player. I felt perspiration trickle down my back and soak my third shirt of the day. Elizabeth Pike was sitting on an overstuffed settee with her eyes closed, lost in the majesty of the music. On a low table in front of her was a glass of clear liquid over ice and a slice of lemon. She was dressed all in black again – a severely cut dress, buttoned to her neck, with black stockings and shoes similar to the ones she had worn to my office. Her hair was combed into a more gentle style than earlier, and it suited her better.

I closed the door behind me with more force than was really necessary and as it slammed she opened her eyes. They were still the saddest, bluest things I'd ever seen. She rose in one graceful move and came to greet me.

'Mr Sharman. Good evening. Let me turn the music off. I often listen at this time of day. This was my father's favourite piece.' She worked a lever at the side of the turntable and the playing arm ejected itself with a mechanical click. It was very quiet in the conservatory then. The sound of traffic from Park Lane was hardly a murmur. 'Would you care for a drink?'

'A vodka and tonic would be good.'

She went to the bar and rattled ice cubes into a glass, added a slice of lemon without asking, poured a good measure of vodka over them, and topped up the glass with tonic water. I took the glass from her and picked up the photograph with the other hand.

'My mother and father,' said Elizabeth. She glanced at her

watch. 'Catherine will be joining us shortly. Please take good care of her. My father would have wanted that.'

I nodded and heard footsteps from the hall outside and we both turned towards the door. It opened and I got my first sight of Catherine Pike in the flesh.

And what a sight it was.

The brief glimpse of her on the TV news hadn't prepared me for the reality of the woman who entered the room.

She was tall and built like your wildest dream come true. Her hair was blonde but mere words couldn't describe it. It was tangled like the sheets on a bed where you'd just had the best fuck of your life. It probably cost a hundred quid to get it to look as untamed as it did. As she stepped into the early evening sunlight pouring through the conservatory windows it took the colour of the sun and became the sun and lit the room like a super nova. It was so bright I could almost feel the heat.

She was wearing black too, but on her it looked more like a challenge than the colour of mourning. Her dress was short and tight, pulled off her shoulders, cut low to show off the tops of her breasts, and hugged her figure without a wrinkle. With the dress she wore sheer black stockings. By contrast, on her feet were a pair of savage pink Joan Crawford fuck-me shoes. The heels were high, five or six inches, and the toes were pointed like needles. Her skin was smooth and creamy and her eyes were blue. Almost the same colour as Elizabeth's and her mother's. I guessed that the eyes of Joanna Bennett with two 't's had been similar. Obviously old Sir Robert went for blue eyes in a big way.

'Catherine,' said Elizabeth, 'this is Nick Sharman. He will be staying with us for the foreseeable future. Mr Sharman, this is my sister Catherine.'

'Hello, Mr Sharman.' Catherine shook my hand. Her voice was deep and melodic, without a trace of accent, and her grip was firm and strong. But I got the feeling that as beautiful, and as beautifully groomed as she was, all was not right with her. I felt that she was keeping as firm a grip on herself as she was on my hand.

'Good evening, Miss Pike,' I said.

Close up she showed more signs of stress. Under her expertly applied make-up there were lines of strain at the corners of her eyes, and I thought I could detect the hint of dark shadows under them. Was she just grieving the loss of a recently found father or was there, as Elizabeth had suggested, more to it than that?

'It's been a terrible time,' she said and finally let go of my hand. 'Liz spoke to me about …' She hesitated. 'Employing you, and I'm glad you're here.'

It was the first I'd heard about it and I looked at Elizabeth. 'I got the impression I might not be very welcome, sticking my nose into such a recent tragedy.'

'On the contrary,' said Catherine. 'I'm sure we both feel much better now you're here.'

'Thank you.' I took a whack at the vodka and tonic.

'Right,' said Elizabeth and picked up her handbag. 'Now that you two have met, I must be going. I have some last-minute arrangements to make for this evening, if I can track down the incompetents who are supposed to be working for us. I'll meet you both at the Crypt later. Can you try to be there early, Catherine?'

'Certainly. I'm sure that Mr Sharman will get me there in plenty of time if all you say about him is true.'

'Of course he will,' said Elizabeth as if it had only just occurred to her. 'You're in good hands. Until later then.' And she left the room.

'Can I get you something to drink, Miss Pike?' I asked.

'Please call me Catherine,' she said. 'And may I call you Nick?'

I nodded. 'Catherine it is then.' Saying her Christian name was like tasting cream.

'I'd love a drink. I'll have a gin.'

I did the honours. I poured her a large, cold one.

'I must apologise for this,' she said. 'But as we're eating out and going on, Liz let the servants have the evening off. I'm sorry we're having to rough it.'

Roughing it. I had to smile. It was about as rough as one of her nylons on a freshly waxed leg.

'I've booked a table at Mr Chow's. I hope that's all right.'

It was fine by me. I've always been partial to a Chinese. 'Great,' I said.

She looked straight into my eyes for a moment. 'I really am glad you're here.'

'Are you? Why?'

'Because there's something … ' She paused.

'Something you think I should know?'

'Yes.'

'What?'

She raised her glass and took a drink. 'But I'm not sure … ' She stopped again, and suddenly looked scared. She moved slightly, and I couldn't see her eyes for the light bursting through the glass behind her, making her the only solid thing in the room. Solid shadow, but that's the only kind I know.

I moved round so that I could see her features but the moment and the words had gone.

She looked at her watch and, as you do, I looked at mine. It was six forty. As if on cue there was a discreet knock at the door and Vincent entered carrying a black silk evening coat which he laid carefully on the sofa.

'The car is ready, miss.' He looked at me as if I was a stubborn stain on its upholstery.

'We'll be right down.'

Vincent backed out of the room and I drained my glass. Catherine picked up the coat and stood holding it. I took it from her and helped her into it. I could smell her perfume like fresh flowers in the hot air. But even in the heat I saw goose pimples on her skin and as my hand brushed her arm I felt their relatives rise on mine. I wondered if she was really scared, and if she was, of what, or whom.

She looked over her shoulder and gave me a half-smile through her thick yellow hair and my goose pimples got goose pimples of their own.

'The car is in the basement,' she said. She walked in front of me as far as the door, then turned. 'Do I look all right?'

'You look just fine.'

'Do you approve of my new shoes?'

'Yes,' I said, then hesitated. I didn't know quite how to put it.

'Oh, the colour,' she said. 'But we are going to a party, and you must remember, Nick, life goes on. My father wouldn't want us to mourn for ever. It wasn't his style.'

With that she swept through the door and I followed her.

We walked together to the lift and it dropped us into the fluorescently lit parking bay where the Rolls-Royce was waiting, idling gently, its exhaust fumes being dragged straight out by the ventilator fans to pollute the street. The bay was about sixty foot square and must once have been part of the cellars. It was low-ceilinged and echoed with our footsteps.

Vincent sprang to open the car door and I followed Catherine from air-conditioning to air-conditioning. It looked like I wouldn't be breathing much London air as long as I kept this job.

Vincent drove to the bottom of a steep ramp and operated a switch on the dash. At the top of the ramp a corrugated metal door slid smoothly into the ceiling. Vincent touched the accelerator and the great car surged up the ramp. He swung it into a narrow mews at the back of the house, then left and left again into Curzon Street.

We arrived in Knightsbridge at seven on the dot. We stepped from the cool of the Rolls into the heat of the street, then straight into air-conditioning again through the door of the restaurant. Much more of those kind of temperature fluctuations and I'd get the flu.

We were met at the door by a Chinese geezer with an LA accent and shown to a table that was just far enough from the kitchen and the loos and just close enough to the window and the bar to make it the best in the place.

Although it was early, the restaurant was already buzzing and the staff were turning away casual punters. We were given a table for four as if it was our right, and I guess it was. The other two settings were cleared without a murmur. I figured that when Catherine wanted a bit of elbow room that was precisely what she got.

She ordered a large gin martini for herself and a vodka martini for me. I didn't argue, but if she was trying to keep me alert she wasn't making a very good job of it.

'Are you hungry?'

'I could be,' I replied.

'Good, I love the food here and I always get far too much. Would you like to order?' she asked me as if I was her escort rather than an employee.

'No,' I said. 'Surprise me.'

'I just might,' she told me with a grin that made her look like a teenager.

She went right through the card from first to last, sesame toast to toffee apples. I was glad I was hungry as dish after delicate dish started arriving, steaming and sizzling from the kitchens. Now I knew why we'd been given a table for four. We piled our bowls full of food and dived in, chopsticks rubbing together like crickets' legs. Catherine ordered a bottle of Meursault to chase the dumplings down and we dived into that too. And when that was gone, she ordered another. We ploughed through course after course of the finest Pekinese cuisine. My head was beginning to swim from too much rich food and booze and I knew that we were still in for a long night. I'd probably regret it by morning, but what the hell.

We finished up with coffee and liqueurs and by that time I was well loaded.

She wasn't doing too badly herself. As we ate and drank, we talked. And the more she sucked up the liquor, the more she told me, which suited me fine. I wanted to hear her side of the story. At first we talked about generalities and then specifics, and her situation in particular. 'Did Liz tell you about me?' she asked, as she dipped into a dish of prawns in black bean sauce.

'Some,' I said. 'Some I knew.'

'And what do you think you knew about me, Nick? Tell me, I'm interested.'

'Only what I read in the papers.'

'You shouldn't believe everything you read in them.'

'Not even Pike papers?' I asked.

'I'll leave you to work that out for yourself. So go on, tell me what you know about me.'

'Very little really.'

'Don't be embarrassed.'

'I'm not.'

'Well then?'

She'd asked for it, so I gave it to her. 'You're Sir Robert Pike's illegitimate daughter,' I said. 'Your mother was sent to Australia when she was pregnant, with instructions never to return. You lived together in hotels until she died. You vanished, then turned up in London where your father accepted you into the bosom of his family, where you've been ever since. End of story.'

'A very short history of my life. You left out a lot. Would you like me to fill in some of the details?'

'Not if it upsets you.'

'It does. But I'll tell you anyway.'

'Only if you want to.'

'I do, then I'll tell you why I'm so glad you're here.'

'Go ahead,' I said. 'I'm listening.'

'It was a very strange childhood. Hardly a childhood at all. Solitary, but always surrounded by people, grown-ups mostly. You were right about the hotel bit. From the time I was born until my mother died we never lived in a house, or even an apartment. Always hotels. Always moving. Eating room-service meals and having the beds made and towels changed for us. I don't think my mother ever saw the inside of a supermarket. She only shopped for clothes. I was always around grown-ups, so I grew up fast. The only other children I ever met were hotel brats themselves. They weren't the kind of hotels where normal children stayed. They were expensive, five star. My father looked after my mother very well financially. I've seen her bank statements. There was always an annual increase to take in inflation and the fact that I was getting older. But my mother was a good spender, I'll give her that. She drank, you see, and you can spend an awful lot in hotel bars.'

'What about school?' I asked.

'School.' She laughed. 'I never went. My mother was too drunk to make me. I hardly even registered. I would go a few times, then quit. The other kids seemed so juvenile, babyish. If the school boards got interested, we moved. Australia is a big place.'

'But you must have had some kind of education.'

'I educated myself. My mother taught me to read before she got too bad. I read the papers, and you'd be amazed the number of books you can find in a first-class hotel. I read *Valley of the Dolls* when I was eight, Anais Nin when I was ten, and as for Stephen King, Christ, I know his stuff backwards.'

'And you kept a scrapbook.'

'How the hell do you know about that? You certainly didn't read about it in the newspapers. I suppose Elizabeth told you. Yes, my mother started it. She hated my father, and I think she collected scraps about him to feed the hatred. She soon forgot about it, though, and I kept it up. There was never a vast amount. He never went to Australia. Guess why? But the hotels generally had English and American papers. I got quite a lot in the end.'

'Did you hate him too?' I asked.

'No. He kept me in luxury. I wasn't crazy about him. I saw what he'd done to my mother but I didn't really understand. She never stopped though. What with that, and the drink, and the men, she ended up hating herself I think.'

'Men?'

'Oh, there were lots. She was an attractive woman until the end, and there are plenty of lonely men in hotels.'

She smoked continuously between courses as she spoke, stubbing out half-smoked cigarettes into the ashtray. When she wasn't smoking or eating or knocking back glasses of booze, she sat twisting her napkin in both hands. I sat opposite her, quietly, letting her tell her story in her own time.

'It sounds bad.'

'It was.'

'You don't have to tell me any more.' I could see that poor little kid, all alone in a mausoleum of a hotel with only a drunk for company, cutting out articles about a man she'd never met.

'It's all right,' she said. 'There's not much more. Then my mother died, and I flipped out. I'd seen drugs around since I was so big. My mother smoked dope to mellow out the booze. I can't remember when I first stole a drink, but I had my first joint when I was eleven. First coke at fourteen. First smack at sixteen. I lost my virginity when I was twelve and by the time Mother died I was strung out like forty miles of bad road. I got worse, then I got better. I wanted to be an actress. I wanted to lose that bloody Australian accent I'd picked up from the lowlifes around, and speak like my mother. I wanted to work in England and meet my father as an equal. So I went to drama school.'

'Just like that?'

'No, not just like that. I'd had no formal education, no bits of paper. I had to suck some dick to get in, but get in I did. I'd vowed not to touch the money that my father had left in my mother's bank account for me, but I needed it for the exorbitant fees. After I graduated I came to London to meet him and pay the money back.'

'And?'

'And I took to the old sod,' she said and tears filled her eyes. 'But I was never going to be a great actress, not like I wanted to be. And my father was so generous, in the end I found it easier to move into Curzon Street with the family when they were staying there, and the castle when they weren't.'

'Castle?'

'Yes, the castle in Hampshire. At Gun Street. The family spends part of the year there, or they used to before my father died. I don't know what will happen now.'

'An honest to God castle?' I persisted.

'Yes, twelfth century.'

I was definitely impressed. 'And now something's wrong,' I said. 'Apart from the obvious.'

'Yes. Since my father died, someone's been calling me on the telephone.'

'Who?'

'I haven't the faintest idea.'

'What kind of calls?'

'Threatening, I suppose you'd say.'

'Threatening what?'

'That unless I paid whoever's calling a lot of money, he'd kill me.'

'And you've no idea who's making these calls?'

'No.'

'Does the name Lorimar mean anything to you?'

She thought about it without a spark of recognition. 'Apart from the production company that makes *Dallas*, no. Why?'

'No reason,' I said.

'So that's why I'm so glad you're here.'

'You haven't told Elizabeth?'

'No, but I know she's guessed something is wrong. She told me about you, and who you are, and how you'd met.'

'You know about that?' I asked.

'Yes, I'm afraid it was rather my fault. I taught her, you see. The girl was so straight when I met her. I started shoplifting a long time ago. Hotel shops are so easy to rob. I had plenty of practice. Is that awful?'

'I'm not exactly Snow White myself.'

'I know. I knew you'd understand. Anyway, when Liz told me about your meeting, and showed me your card, I sort of put in her head to go and see you. I hope I didn't do wrong.'

'It would have been handy to know there were death threats involved,' I said.

'That's why we're dining alone tonight, Nick. Normally Liz would have been here whether she had things to do or not. But I convinced her that it would be better tête-à-tête, as it were.'

'I'm sure you can be very convincing,' I said.

'I'd do anything to convince you to protect me from whoever's making these threats.'

'Anything?' I asked.

'Anything in the world you can think of.' And her hand fluttered on my arm and her eyelashes fluttered over her beautiful blue eyes.

'Catherine, I think you've got a deal,' I said.

'Will you promise?' she asked.

I smiled. I felt a bit like a yo-yo on the end of a piece of string. 'Of course,' I said, and changed the subject. 'Hadn't we better go soon? You're supposed to be at the reception early.'

She looked at her watch. 'Yes, you're right. Will you get the bill, please?'

I attracted the attention of the greeter and he conjured up the waiter who conjured up the bill which was about as long as the invoice for the Great Wall of China. Catherine paid with a gold Amex and no trace of embarrassment. A new woman if ever I saw one. I let her pay with no trace of embarrassment either. I was more than eager to be a new man.

She left a tip that would have paid for a decent meal at my

favourite local Chinese and the waiter brought her card and her coat. I let him help her put it on, told her to wait for a minute and went looking for Vincent. He was parked on a bus stop opposite the restaurant. I waved him over with a rather more imperious gesture than was really necessary, and I saw his lips move through the open window as he drove across through a gap in the traffic. When he pulled up I told him to stay where he was and went back for Catherine. I led her from the chill of the restaurant through the thick atmosphere of the late evening and into the passenger compartment of the freezing car. Flu was a certainty, and a spot of indigestion from too many noodles a distinct possibility. I hurried her to the car like I imagined heavy-duty bodyguards treat their charges. I didn't really expect anything to happen, but I was being paid for my time and Catherine had paid for the dinner so I thought I'd better do something in exchange for the meal.

I climbed aboard and sat on the fold-down seat facing her. We drove with the park on our left, through the underpass at Hyde Park Corner, down Piccadilly, swung left into Shaftesbury Avenue, left again into Wardour Street, then right at Compton Street and into Dean Street. It was just before ten when we slid to a halt opposite the Crypt and nearly full dark, although the air had that luminous look that it sometimes gets in London in summer as the day's heat rises from the pavements.

I checked the street through the tinted glass, opened the door, stepped out into the night and soaked my shirt again. I swear it was getting hotter as the night got older.

I helped Catherine out of the car, feeling her breast touch my arm briefly, and walked her across the pavement towards the entrance to the club. There were cars parked down both sides of the street and suddenly a dark, male figure sprang up from behind one, right into our path. Catherine screamed and turned towards me in terror. I saw that the man was holding something in his hand with a pistol grip. It was all confusion for a moment. The street was crowded and people were stopping and bumping into each other to see what all the excitement was about. I grabbed Catherine and pushed her out of my way. I saw her almost fall in those ridiculous shoes. I straight-armed the geezer and I heard him gasp as I hit him. I tugged whatever he was carrying out of his hand and threw it across the pavement, then I spun him round and ran him hard up against the closest wall with a satisfying crunch. I put an arm lock on him and forced him down to his knees. I heard the skin peeling from his face as it ran down the brickwork. It all took less than five seconds. I heard the door of the Rolls slam and Vincent's boots pound on the road as he ran across to see what was going on. I held my man down, then Vincent said, 'I think you'd better let him go.'

I eased off and whoever I was holding moaned in pain. I looked round and Vincent was standing, holding a camera in his hand. He pressed a button and a repeater flash went off like a strobe light. I felt like a complete berk and Vincent knew it. 'Fancied a snap, did you?' he asked softly.

And that was that. I helped the paparazzi to his feet and tried my best to dust him down. His face was a mess, it was bloody and starting to bruise and his dignity was in about the same shape. I stood there sweating in a mixture of heat and embarrassment in front of the gawping crowd.

Catherine pushed through and I turned to explain.

'Nick, are you all right?' she gasped. 'Oh, you were wonderful. I was so frightened. I thought that man had a gun.' She turned on the photographer. 'For whom do you work?' she demanded. Thank God for elocution classes, I thought.

'I'm freelance, Miss Pike,' he said.

'I think you'd better send me the bill personally for any damages.' Then she leant closer so that only the four of us could hear, and said in pure Australian, 'But don't try and stitch me up or you'll be chasing me through the courts for ever, or maybe I'll send Nick here to pay you a visit, you little cunt.'

The look on his face was beautiful, and it was mirrored on Vincent's. I realised what she had meant when she said she'd grown up fast. Fast and tough, a real chip off the old block. I'm sure Sir Robert would have been proud of her. I walked over and took the camera from Vincent's grasp and gave it back to the photographer.

The Roller was blocking the street and there were drivers freaking out all the way back to Cambridge Circus. I turned to Vincent and said, 'You'd better move on. I'll give you a call on the car phone when we need you.'

He gave me a look of pure disgust as he walked away. I shrugged and turned and followed Catherine into the club where Elizabeth was standing by the reception desk, tapping her fingernails on the top. I could see that she was well pissed off.

'I'm going to the loo to repair my face,' said Catherine. 'Why don't you look after Liz. She looks as if her knicker elastic just broke.'

I could see what she meant. 'Okay,' I said. 'I'll catch you up.'

'You'll find me in the bar,' said Catherine and wobbled off on her spikes. I went over to Elizabeth Pike.

'What's the story?' I asked, although all I really wanted to know was the location of the bar.

'That prick Barrington hasn't shown and the people here aren't happy.'

'Who's Barrington?' I asked.

'The PR for the magazine.'

'Where is he?'

'How the hell do I know? You're the detective. You tell me.'

'I love it when you scold me,' I said.

'No silly jokes, Mr Sharman. This is serious. And what the hell was going on outside?'

I explained and she shook her head. I thought I was due a scolding again, but suddenly there was a big commotion at the door and a tall, skinny geezer came bursting through dragging a pretty brunette behind him. I looked at Elizabeth.

'Barrington?'

The look on her face was answer enough.

6

The publicist was a long-haired article whose locks had been caught up in an elastic band and pulled tightly back into a single bunch. Personally I've always had great difficulty relating to mature men with ponytails, but that's my problem. What's more, he was wearing a better suit than mine, his shirt had cost twenty quid more than my shirt, and his tie had cost more than my shirt alone. Even the shine on his shoes made my heart ache, so I concentrated on the girl who had come in with him. She was a real blinder, not very tall, but with a figure that could knock your eyes out and a mane of hair as black as the inside of a crow's eyelid that reached almost down to her waist. She wasn't trying to hide her light under a bushel either. The dress she was wearing was a shiny, ruched number in electric blue. It was tighter than a sausage skin, well off the shoulder and ended up just below her crotch.

'Down, boy,' said Elizabeth.

'Just keeping an eye out for concealed weapons.'

She gave me a look that could have peeled paint. I gave her a boyish grin back, but somehow lately I think my boyishness is wearing a bit thin.

'I'd better get on with my job,' I said.

She nodded and turned to the publicist. 'Barrington!' she yelled. 'Get into the bar, now.'

'Hello, boss,' said Barrington. 'I'll take a rain check on the drinky if you don't mind, I'm a bit late and there's masses to do,'

'No drinky, Barrington. Talky. And right now. I don't want to talk to you out here. I want some privacy.'

Barrington pulled a face and followed her through to the bar where staff were still putting the finishing touches to the preparations for the reception.

'And leave the bimbo behind. This is business,' said the guv'nor over her shoulder as she went.

I turned and looked at the brunette who'd arrived with Barrington. She returned my look and said, 'Don't take it too much to heart. I'm sure she'll let you in later.'

I gave her another look. 'Not bad,' I said. 'Off the cuff. Why don't we leave them to it and get a drink? I'm sure we can find a corner out of their way.'

'Yeah, all right, why not?'

'I'll take care of this young lady,' I said to Elizabeth's and Barrington's retreating backs. They ignored me. I shrugged and pulled a face at the girl. 'Do you think that means they approve of the idea?'

'Couldn't give a fuck. Just lead me to the juice.'

The more I saw of this girl, the more I liked her.

We walked together to the bar. 'What do you want?'

'A cottage in the country and a BMW,' she replied. 'What the fuck do you think I want? Something to get me off, of course.'

A right shrinking violet, I thought. 'Anything in particular or shall I amaze you with my powers of perspicacity?'

'Is that like Malibu?'

'Better and better,' I said. 'Do you go into training for this?'

For the first time she cracked her face and gave me a view of her teeth. 'No, it just comes naturally. I'll have a Killer Zombie.'

I beckoned the barman over. He was a muscular clone, all brush cut and big moustache, wearing a white shirt, bow tie and black pants so tight you could see his appendix scar. 'A Killer Zombie please and a pint of mild for my mother,' I said. The girl gave me a tight-faced, deadpan smile.

The barman didn't smile at all. 'I'm sorry, sir, we don't serve mild ale.'

'Make it a large vodka and orange juice instead.'

'A Killer Zombie and a large Screwdriver,' he said. 'Yes, sir.'

While he was preparing the drinks, I turned back to the girl and asked her name.

'Fiona.'

'Are you with him?'

'Who?'

'Barrington,' I replied patiently.

'What do you mean, with him?'

'Is he your boy friend?'

'Piss off ... that prat? Not likely. I'm working here tonight.'

'Doing what?'

'Don't you know?'

'No.'

'Are you kidding me?'

'No.'

'You really don't know what I do?'

'No.'

'This,' she said, and tugged the ruched top of her dress down to her waist exposing her breasts. I didn't know quite where to look. It seemed that everywhere I went that day women were flashing their flesh at me.

'Oh,' I said.

'Page three,' she explained. 'I'm a topless model. I'm famous.'

'Oh,' I said again. The barman who was just bringing our drinks didn't turn a hair. He'd probably rather have seen my chest. She pulled the top of her dress up again and wriggled around until it was comfortable, then dumped the umbrella and fruit and plastic crap in her drink in a sticky mess on the top of the bar and sank half of it in one gulp.

'I'd better have another two of those,' I said to the barman. 'And bring me another vodka while you're at it.'

He went off to do as he was told and out of the corner of my eye I saw Elizabeth giving me the evil eye from down the bar where she was talking to Barrington.

'I'll remember next time,' I said.

'Yeah, you'd better. I'm in the *Sun* tomorrow.'

'I'll be sure to buy a copy. Perhaps you can autograph it for me.'

'What?'

'The paper.'

'Oh, is that all?'

'For now.'

'What's your name then?' Fiona asked.

'Nick.'

'What do you do?'

'Not a lot,' I replied.

She looked me up and down. 'I can imagine. What are you doing here, then?'

It was a good question, and I improvised. 'I'm doing a spot of work on behalf of Sir Robert Pike's estate, and as I'm staying at the Pikes' house they invited me along.' It wasn't a lie, but it wasn't the whole truth.

'Christ, you're privileged.'

'Am I?'

'Maybe not. The old boy was okay. I met him a couple of times. It was a shame about him. But the kids, not a patch. They're a stuck-up lot.'

'Are they?'

'You heard the way Miss Elizabeth,' she heavily accentuated the word "Miss", 'spoke to Barrington. There was no need for that. He's not so bad. A bit of a pain maybe. But I'll tell you this, he could handle one of these thrashes in his sleep. And the other one, Miss Catherine, ain't much better.' She stopped and looked at me hard. 'You're not knocking one of them off, are you?'

'No, nothing like that.'

'Thank Christ for that. Me and Barrington are in enough trouble as it is, without me putting my big foot in it.' She lurched closer to me and I saw that the pupils of her eyes were as big as saucers. 'You wouldn't have any luck with that Elizabeth anyway, from what I hear, but the other, the blonde. You could be all right with her.'

'Is that so?'

'So they say.'

'Who says?'

She winked. 'All sorts. I get around and so does she. But I'm being naughty.' She touched the lapel of my jacket. 'Perhaps I'm jealous.'

'What of?'

'Of you with her.'

I could feel myself starting to warm up. 'Don't wind me up, Fiona,' I said. 'I didn't just pop out of an egg.'

'I bet you didn't. If I didn't know better I'd say you were Old Bill.'

Too close for comfort. Then, like the cavalry to the rescue, Catherine came out of the loo and made towards us, the barman brought our extra drinks, and Barrington headed our way. 'Here we go,' said Fiona. 'Looks like I'm wanted. I'd better go and change. I'll see you later.'

'I'll look forward to it,' I said.

'Thanks for the drink.'

'It was a pleasure.'

She pulled a wry face and headed Barrington off at the pass and they went together to the back of the club.

Catherine arrived as Fiona left. They didn't acknowledge each other. I should have known from the start they weren't soul mates.

I took a hit off my new vodka. 'Common little cow,' said Catherine.

'She seemed all right to me. Do you want a drink?' I felt more like a cocktail waiter than a private detective.

'Gin, please, large.'

'You didn't have to say,' I muttered under my breath as I passed the order onto the barman.

Then Elizabeth joined us. 'Get me something, please,' she instructed. See what I mean? 'That guy is such a fuck-up, I can hardly believe he's still in business.'

'What's the problem?' I asked solicitously as I beckoned the barman over again and ordered another large gin and tonic.

'Just the usual. Lack of communication. I should have kept a closer eye on Barrington. It's my fault, I've let things slip. He's snorting coke over in the Zanzibar with that little scrubber when he should have been here sorting out the guest list. And that's another thing. The guest list. It's just a load of Barrington's broken-down old ligger mates. I told him I wanted A and B people who'd get this reception into the papers and get the magazine some good publicity, and he comes up with every loser in town. I just hope we get some good press people down here or he's out.'

Down or out, I thought, but said nothing.

The barman brought the drinks and Elizabeth took a miserable sip of hers. 'I wouldn't mind, but Daddy so wanted this magazine to succeed.'

Catherine touched her arm, 'It will, you've done a wonderful job.' I almost expected a "there, there" from the look on her face.

'Are the drinks free?' I asked.

'All night,' Elizabeth said.

'You'll be all right then.'

'Thanks Mr Sharman,' she said, covering my hand with hers. 'I wish it were that simple.' There was so much touching going on I thought we might contact Sir Robert on the other side and ask him ourselves.

The first of the guests started dribbling in around about then. I don't know much about A and B people, although I guessed that I'd comfortably fit somewhere between X and Z. But this crew didn't strike me as exactly the cream of the glitterati. The first few crept through the door clutching their free copies of the new magazine and looking about as happy as the Jackson Five getting ready to entertain a Ku Klux Klan convention. Catherine went back to the loo. Weak bladder? Maybe, maybe not.

'Jesus,' said Elizabeth, disturbing my reverie. 'Where did he dig these turkeys up?'

'Early days,' I said. 'Why don't you circulate and give the hoi polloi the benefit of your charm and poise? Don't worry, I won't be far away. And listen, I've got to talk to you soon. Catherine's been telling me some things.'

'Like what?'

'I can't tell you now, later maybe.'

'I won't be through until after this is all over. How about tomorrow?'

'Tomorrow morning, first thing?'

'As first thing as I can.'

'It's important.'

'All right, Mr Sharman, first thing tomorrow it is, I promise.'

Catherine came out of the Ladies'. Elizabeth grabbed her and they were immediately pounced upon by a pair of Gerrard Street smoothies who looked like they were flogging a frozen prawn franchise. I hesitated, but Elizabeth shrugged and made a pushing motion with her hands so I left them to it.

The place was filling up. The prospect of free food and drink was dragging the movers and shakers away from the TV and their usual haunts to check out the first edition of *Cause Célèbre*. A couple of chefs in tall hats were getting ready to dish out a sumptuous-looking buffet from a long table at the back of the restaurant and several waiters were working the crowd with trays of champagne in fluted glasses. It was all very smooth and sophisticated, but the whole set-up made me distinctly uncomfortable.

I exchanged my empty vodka glass for a full one of champagne, wedged myself in a quiet corner, parked the glass on a ledge, lit a cigarette and gave the party my full attention. By then the room was about a quarter full. The air-conditioning was coping and after the heat outside the temperature was a pleasant seventy or so. A couple of guys had set up a mobile sound system in one corner and were playing a selection of forties and fifties bop and stroll records at a volume that got the music across without being intrusive. It was that kind of function.

Barrington and Fiona were holding court at a table that had been set up at the main door and was piled high with copies of the magazine. Fiona had changed into an even more minute mini dress, if that was possible. This one was crimson red and slashed dramatically to the navel. I wondered if Brunel had a copyright on her underwear. It was an enticing thought.

People were moving around as if dancing a complicated gavotte. Little groups formed and dissolved in front of my eyes; the champagne was making my head sweat. I listened a lot and said little. A few people gave me the once-over, a couple made noncommittal comments. I spoke when I was spoken to, but didn't make much of an effort. It wasn't difficult. The state of some of the characters I clocked could curdle your Piña Colada, and all they talked about was money, money, money.

Like I said, I listened a lot and it didn't take me long to work out the pecking order in the magazine publishing world. It appeared to be mostly run by women, and they soon separated into three distinct types. At the bottom were the younger women. Slabs of blonde hair, big bins, small breasts, mini skirts and dark tights. The middle echelon were dumpy Sloanes with voices that could rupture an eardrum at forty paces. They had the monopoly on bad legs, silk sweeps from Hermès, and Liberty print blouses so muddy I was looking for bullfrogs in their cleavages. And at the top were tall, skinny women with hair like glass fibre, power suits with shoulder pads and the kind of predatory look that made you think that if they gave you a blow job you might not get your dick back at the end of it. Their escorts were an eclectic mixture of Hooray Henrys, tattooed love boys and suburban social workers in Kicker boots. Nice people, one and all. They made me want to puke my bean sprout and sesame salad.

After about an hour of moving around and earwigging I thought it was about time I found Catherine again. I made for the main bar, but got hung up outside, where a giggle of hairdressers had congregated. They were discussing scissors and gel and perm lotion and other important stuff. They were checking out hair styles and looking for thin patches in the passing bouffants. Suddenly a little spat seemed to flare up and one particular peacock, a dream in black satin and platform soles, broke away from the pack and headed towards me in an unsteady fashion. He gripped my arm with a surprisingly strong fist and gave me the full benefit of his baby blues. 'Fancy a line, sweet?'

I removed his hand and smoothed down the sleeve of my jacket. 'A line of what?' I asked innocently.

He giggled and rubbed his face, smudging his eyeliner. 'Don't kid a kidder,' he whispered. 'Let's make a break for the Gents'.'

'What about your pals?'

He sniffed as if it hadn't been just cocaine that had got up his nose. 'Those bitches,' he said, 'can kiss my arse for a hit on my drugs. I'd rather share with a real man.'

I felt complimented. 'Sorry,' I said. 'Not right now. I'm looking for the young lady I came with.'

'Oh,' he said, concealing a tiny burp with the back of his hand. 'Do tell, who could that possibly be?'

'Catherine Pike.'

I thought he was going to have a fit. He danced from one foot to the other; then, all hard feelings forgotten, he dragged his chums over and after getting my name from me and making introductions all round, explained my situation to them.

'So you're the latest,' said a tall boy with an Egyptian look and the unlikely name of Ivan. 'I must say she's going severely down market.'

'She always did like a bit of rough,' said my original acquaintance, whose name was Leee, with three vowels. He saw the look on my face. 'Now don't be offended. We're only teasing and, speaking for myself, just a teensy weensy bit jealous. We've all been remarking on you since we came in, and dying for you to join us, and now we find you're spoken for. And with Catherine of all people, and she never even told me.'

'Why should she?' I asked.

'Who do you think is responsible for making the lovely Cathy's coiffure the talk of the place?' He pouted. 'Every hair cries "Leee". I'm her personal stylist. She doesn't touch a shampoo bottle without first consulting me. And everybody knows what an intimate relationship a girl has with her hairdresser. So I insist you tell me everything about yourself, Nicholas. I spy an empty table over there, and I'm gasping for a Cuba Libra. Be a dear and get me one from the bar, and we can have a lovely chat.'

We left the other hairdressers bitching about being excluded, and while Leee captured the table, I went to the bar and ordered a large rum and Coca-Cola and a vodka for myself. As I expected, Catherine was there, surrounded by a small fan club. She seemed to be in good hands so I left her to it. Elizabeth was nowhere to be seen.

When the drinks arrived I carried them back to the table and sat next to Leee. He tasted his drink and lit one of my cigarettes.

'Right, Nicholas dear,' he said. 'Tell me all.'

I decided to stick to the story I'd told Fiona. 'There's not much to tell,' I said. 'I'm doing some work on Sir Robert's estate. Nothing special. Just collating a few papers. I'm staying at Curzon Street until I finish, and Miss Pike invited me to dinner and then on here. It's not very interesting, I'm afraid.' I smiled, and the smile was full of modesty and sincerity. I practise it every morning in the mirror when I'm shaving.

'Catherine's boy friends are always interesting,' said Leee. 'Such a fascinating assortment of types.'

'Rough trade, I think you said.'

'Oh, Nicholas, I told you I was only teasing, but I could tell you some tales.'

'I'll just bet you could.'

'And perhaps I will.' He grinned, and I knew he would spill the beans in his own time.

'How long have you known her?' I asked.

'I met her the first day she was in London. She came in for a shampoo and set.' He grinned again. 'I styled her hair. We got talking. We've been talking ever since. I do her hair once or twice a week. She can afford it. Rich people talk to their hairdressers. I read between the lines. I listen between the words.' He tapped his forehead. 'You don't have to be very suss to get the message.'

'So tell me about her other men.'

He took a long swallow of his drink, and spat ice back into the glass. 'I swear you're jealous, Nicholas,' he said.

'I'm just an employee of the family. I don't sleep with her. Why should I be jealous?' But I believe I was, just a bit.

'But you'd like to,' said Leee. 'I know the symptoms. And I bet she's already let you know she's available.'

I shrugged and he cracked up.

'Beware, my dear,' he said. 'If Catherine was a narcotic, she'd be Class A under the Dangerous Drugs Act. Men tend to OD on her. I've seen them wandering, two steps behind her, glassy-eyed and confused. A little of her can go a long way, and she rarely gives only a little at a time, But I warn you, she tends to get bored and withhold privileges, so step carefully or it could end in tears.'

'I'll survive.'

'You may or you may not, we shall see. There have been a lot who haven't.'

'Is that right?'

'Nicholas, you're sounding less and less like, what was it? A collator, and more like, well, I'm not sure what.'

I'd have to watch that. 'I'm just interested,' I said. 'So tell me.'

'Very well, if you insist. There have been plenty. When I met her she knew no one in London. We came to be good friends. I took her round the hotspots.' He laughed out loud at the word. 'We did have some fun. All sorts of fun. We painted the town blood red, my dear Nicholas. The hets swarmed around her like the proverbial bees at the honey pot, and what a sweet little pot she's got, or so I've been told.' He flashed his eyes at me through the curls that tumbled around his forehead. 'Of course I don't know firsthand, but I did get some of her leftovers.'

I glanced up and saw Catherine at the entrance to the bar looking around the room as if searching for someone, and I guessed it might be me.

'Listen,' I said. 'I'd like to talk some more sometime. Can I have your phone number?'

'You rascal, you.'

'Strictly business,' I assured him.

'I bet you say that to all the boys.'

I gave him a sour look and he gave me his telephone number on the back of a card with the name of the salon where he worked on the front. 'Call me any time,' he said.

I told him that I would, and excused myself and went to see Catherine. I guessed she'd soaked up another half-bottle of gin since I'd last seen her, but she seemed pretty fit under the circumstances. 'I see you've met Leee,' she said.

'I could hardly miss him.'

'Watch him, Nick, you're just his type.'

'Thanks, I've already gathered that.'

She giggled and put her hand in front of her mouth to stifle it. 'You are scoring tonight, aren't you? That little tart Fiona what's-her-name, Leee, and I'm left all alone to fend for myself.'

'You seem to be doing all right.'

'I always do. Now I must go to the loo. Will you excuse me?'

'Of course.' I said, and off she went.

I lassoed a waiter and helped myself to another sherbet. I perched on the corner of a handy sofa and thought about all the bits of stories I'd heard that night. I squinted at my watch. It was midnight. Various Cinderellas were shedding their glass slippers and heading off to pastures new but there were still new people arriving and the party showed no signs of slowing down.

Suddenly the crowd in front of me parted and Fiona tumbled through. 'Budge up, Nick, and let me sit down, for Christ's sake, my bloody feet are killing me.'

I concurred with her request and she hitched herself up on the sofa next to me and eased her shoes off. 'That feels good.' She stretched her toes. 'Hold on, I'll be right back.' She walked off barefooted and snagged two glasses of champagne from a waiter, then padded back and rejoined me on the sofa. I accepted one of the drinks from her.

'Cheers,' she said and knocked back a mouthful. 'By fuck, I'm grafting tonight, thank God the other girl's turned up and I can take a break.'

'What are you doing?' I asked.

'Just the usual. Pushing the dumb product on people who only want to get pissed for free. Being nice to silly cunts who only want to look down the front of my dress, letting silly cunts have their picture taken with me, and fighting off their wandering hands.'

'Not interested, huh?'

'Fuck 'em. Like I told you, I'm famous – well, nearly. But I'm a pro now, and I mean pro model.'

'Good,' I said. 'Another rugged individualist, I like that.'

'So do I,' she said. 'It feels so good. Got any fags?'

I fished out a Silk Cut for each of us and she lit them with a Zippo lighter she rescued from the depths of her bag. The lighter was brass and was decorated with an SAS regimental badge in coloured enamel.

'Is he your mate?' she asked.

'Who?'

'Leee, hairdresser to the stars. You two looked pretty tight.'

'No,' I replied.

'You're not gay, are you?'

I knew the colour of the shirt had been a mistake. 'Do I look gay?'

'What does gay look like?' she shot back. 'You'd be amazed. Or would you?'

'Probably,' I said. 'And no, I'm not gay. I just like talking to hairdressers.'

She looked me straight in the eye and said, 'You're a funny cunt, Nick, but I quite like you. Do you fancy getting weird?'

'How weird?'

'Very weird.'

'With what?'

'Nepaleses temple balls.'

I tapped the badge on the lighter. 'Husband?'

'No, dad and brother,'

'Jesus Christ.'

'Well, do you?' she asked again.

'Nothing I'd like more.'

'Come on then.'

'I don't think so.'

'Why not?'

'We might have to get married.'

'I wouldn't mind,' she said. 'On a temporary basis, that is.'

'But would you still respect me in the morning?' I asked.

She giggled. 'Want to find out?'

'Love to, but I think I'd better stay on the straight and narrow tonight. I'm out with the bosses. You know what I mean.' I gave her one of those sincere and modest smiles I'd been practising.

'I do, but it was worth a try, wasn't it?'

'It was worth more than that.'

'Do you want my number?' she asked, and went on, ''course I might not fancy you another night?'

'Want to find out?' I asked, and she grinned and put the lighter back into her bag and felt around inside until she came up with another pasteboard card for my rapidly expanding collection.

'This is my agent,' she said. 'Ring there and leave a number I can get you on. They'll give it to me. If I haven't changed my mind, I'll be in touch. Meanwhile, here's something to be going on with.' She leant over and kissed me on the lips. Her slippery little tongue forced its way into my mouth and touched my teeth. She smelt of White Linen and hot woman, mixed. I reached out for her but she was gone. 'Eat your heart out,' she said, winked, picked up her shoes and made for the ladies' room.

I did just that for a minute. I ate my heart out, then picked myself up and brushed myself down and made for the bar.

That was how the small hours went. The crowd moved round like a carousel. I met some other people whom I can hardly remember through the vodka fog. I spoke to Leee again, and Fiona, and several other people I don't remember.

Eventually I ended up in the bar with Catherine. We were both smashed and sat on a pair of bar stools with our knees touching and swapped sad stories. I remember at one point she was crying and I was pretty close. She went to the Ladies' to repair the damage and came back and told me she wanted to leave. She gave me the number of the car phone in the Rolls and I borrowed the telephone behind the bar and called up Vincent. I told him to meet us out front in fifteen minutes.

She made her goodbyes and we collected her coat and made for the door. I checked with Elizabeth and she told me she would get the company limo to run her home. I wished her good night and left. It was still muggy as hell outside and the city smelled like a used flannel.

I saw the Roller parked on Old Compton and Vincent flashed the headlights, indicated a left turn and pulled out to cross over into Dean Street. Catherine and I walked between two cars to meet him, but before he could turn, a dark-coloured old Marina or Avenger without lights screeched away from the kerb behind the Rolls, swung out round it and turned towards us. I dragged Catherine back and the old banger hit the car beside us and bounced up Dean Street in a flurry of sparks and the smell of burning rubber. Catherine dropped like a stone and I caught her round the waist.

Vincent pulled up in front of us, leaped out and opened the rear door. He helped me to get Catherine into the car and onto the back seat.

'Is she all right?' he asked, with an edge of panic in his voice.

'I think so. Get moving in the direction of a hospital and give me some light in here.'

He jumped back behind the wheel and hit the switch that gave me a reasonable light in the back. Catherine moaned and I felt around for torn clothing or any sign that she'd been hit by the car. It wasn't a bad job and I took my time.

She felt all right, more than all right, and by the time she opened her eyes I was sure she'd simply fainted.

'Are you okay?' I asked.

'You should know,' she said. 'I haven't had an examination like that since the last time I went to my gynaecologist.'

'You're okay.' I tapped on the dividing glass and told Vincent to forget the hospital and take us home.

7

I woke up the next morning alone in a strange bed. It wasn't so bad. It made a change from waking up alone in my own. I felt even more shitty than usual. I'd slept for three hours. At least things were looking up in that direction, I usually barely managed two.

I rolled onto my back. The sun was long up and the room was stifling. I wished I'd switched on the air-conditioning. I crawled out of bed and made for the bathroom. I won't tell you what I looked like. I washed and shaved and found all my clothes hanging neatly in the wardrobe. Thank you, Miranda, I thought and wondered if I'd have to pack them again pretty damn quick after the fiasco of the previous night. I dressed in blue jeans and a big, soft shirt and took a walk around the house to help my hangover. It was as quiet as a wet afternoon in Ongar. I took a flight of stairs down to the basement looking for some life and smelt bacon and coffee and followed my nose and found the kitchen. Miranda was sitting at a huge scrubbed table eating breakfast with a big woman in kitchen whites and an elderly, steel-haired man in a black jacket and striped pants. They all stood up as I entered the kitchen. Miranda looked well fit in her black dress and a fresh apron.

'Good morning,' she said.

'Is it?' I replied.

'As bad as that?'

'Worse.'

'Never mind.'

The two older parties were giving me a good blimp. 'This is Mr Sharman,' said Miranda. 'Mr Sharman, this is Mrs Bishop, our cook, and Mr Courtneidge, the butler.'

I forced a smile. 'Good morning. I'm pleased to meet you. Don't stand up on my account, I only work here – for the moment, anyway.'

They both relaxed and nodded to me and sat back down.

'Do you mind if I join you?' I asked. 'I feel lousy.'

'Of course,' said Courtneidge. 'Please do.'

I sat down at the head of the table.

'Would coffee help?' asked Miranda.

'It might.'

'New Guinea, filter fine, there's a fresh pot brewing.'

'Sounds good.'

'How was the party?' she asked.

'The party was fine.'

'Good, I'm so glad it went well.'

'It had its moments.'

'What time did you get back?'

'Three thirty or so.'

'You're up early.'

'I don't sleep much these days.'

'Why not?'

'When I sleep I dream, and when I dream, I wake up.'

'Always?'

'So far.'

'What do you dream about?'

'Dead people mostly.'

'Why?'

I looked up at her and right into her dark brown eyes. 'Most of the people I've known are dead,' I said.

Her eyes never flinched. 'That sounds very dramatic.'

'It can be.'

Courtneidge and Mrs Bishop witnessed the exchange in silence.

'Do you want some breakfast?' asked Mrs Bishop.

From the dramatic to the mundane in a moment. But then, that's life.

'I'll pass on food for a while, but I'll take the coffee,' I said with as much good grace as I could muster.

Miranda brought me over a breakfast cup full of coffee. It smelt like heaven and tasted like paradise. 'Thank you,' I said and sunk my face into the cup. It was strong, the way I like it, and dark, and sweet as a virgin's kiss. I wondered how many virgins I'd kissed lately, or ever.

When I'd drained the cup Miranda asked me how I felt.

'Better, but still lousy – it's the drink.'

'You shouldn't drink so much,' she said. 'It's bad for you.'

'Miss Elizabeth won't be down for a while. She left a message to be called at eight, and that she wants to see you the minute she's dressed,' said Courtneidge. 'Miss Catherine will be late, I expect.'

'I wouldn't blame her if she was!'

'Are you sure about breakfast?' asked Mrs Bishop.

'Quite sure, but I'll have another cup of coffee, if I may.'

'Of course,' she replied with a smile.

I sat and drank more coffee and watched Miranda's bottom moving under her skirt as she went about her duties. I always watch women's bottoms, have done as long as I can remember. You can't tell anything about their personalities from them, but it sure is a great way to pass the time.

About seven thirty and three cups and ten thousand revolutions later I went for a walk. I needed some air before I got bollocked for nearly losing Catherine. Miranda showed me how to squeeze past the rubbish bins and up some steps and out into the mews at the back of the house. It was warm and sticky out, but the park smelt better in the morning air. I bought a paper and I was in the damn thing. On the gossip page was a picture of Catherine with some pop star halfway down the front of her dress. In the background was half my face neatly sliced by the edge of the photograph. It was hard to tell how I looked, all things considered. There were a few lines about the reception, but nothing about a photographer being assaulted. I guessed Barrington had come good.

I trashed the paper and walked into Hyde Park. There were lots of rich people riding horses and poor people kipping al fresco. In between, there were lots of middle-income people whose dogs were fouling the grass.

I walked on, dodging the shit, through the dapple of light and shade as the sun played hide and seek behind the leaves and branches.

I got back to the house around eight thirty. I sneaked in through the back way again and caught Miranda alone in the kitchen.

'Is she up?' I asked.

'Who?'

'Elizabeth.'

'Miss Elizabeth is in the breakfast room having –'

'Breakfast,' I finished for her.

'That's right.'

'Is there any coffee in there?' I asked.

'A big fresh pot.'

'Great. I'll join her then. By the way, where is the breakfast room? I can't work out the geography of this place at all.'

'Upstairs between the conservatory and the dining room.'

'Jesus,' I said. 'A room for everything and everything has a room.'

She looked at me oddly.

'And thanks again for the livener this morning,' I said. 'You make the best coffee I've tasted in a long while.'

She smiled and showed perfect teeth. I thought for a minute she was going to drop me a curtsy, but she didn't.

'Thank you, sir,' she said. 'But you've got Mrs Bishop to thank for that.'

'I will and please call me Nick. I'll see you later.'

I left the kitchen and headed upstairs through still hallways until I found Elizabeth. She was seated alone at a long table covered with a thick white tablecloth in a sun-filled room, chasing a piece of toast around her plate. She was dressed in a black linen suit without stockings, and black pumps. Her hair hung loosely to her shoulders. She looked pale, but on her it didn't look bad.

'Good morning,' I said.

'I wanted to see you half an hour ago,' she said sharply.

'I was out.'

'Where?'

'Taking a walk, reading about the party in the paper.' I summoned a smile. 'I got my picture in the *Express*, how about that?'

'By Christ, you're cheerful for someone who nearly blew it last night.'

'Mind over matter,' I replied. 'I feel lousy.'

'So do I,' said Elizabeth.

I made no comment, just grabbed a fast cup of coffee and sat down opposite her.

'Catherine, on the other hand, is blooming. She waited up for me last night full of tales of your derring-do. You made quite an impression.'

'I'm pleased to hear it.'

'So what happened?'

'Give me a clue.'

'Did someone try and kill Catherine?'

'Your guess is as good as mine.'

'Why didn't you do something?'

'What could I do? I was too busy looking out for her.'

'So I heard.'

'What does that mean?'

'Nothing.'

'Good.'

'Did you tell the police?'

'Why bother? No one could see the number plate and I was hardly in a position to chase after them.'

'The law might be able to do something,' she said.

'And they might not. They'd say that the driver didn't stop because he or she might have been on the piss or had no insurance or was so stoned that he or she didn't even notice.'

'It was a hell of a thing not to notice,' Elizabeth retorted.

'It happens.'

'But what do you think?' she insisted.

'I think that Catherine put the idea of hiring me into your head because she says she's been on the receiving end of a series of telephone calls threatening to kill her unless she comes across with some cash.'

'What?' she said in a high-pitched voice and her hands flew to her mouth. She cleared her throat and repeated the question in a lower tone of voice.

'You heard,' I said.

'When did she tell you that?'

'Last night, over dinner.'

'She's never told me.'

'She didn't have to. You knew something was up.'

'Yes, I did, didn't I? But why didn't she tell me herself, straight out?'

'I have no idea.'

'But who would want to kill her?'

I shrugged. 'Who knows? Maybe she owes money to someone, and doesn't want to admit it. Has she got any money of her own?'

'I don't know.'

'Come on, Miss Pike,' I said. 'Don't go coy on me. You've already told me you've been through your father's financial records. Did he give her a lot of money as an allowance or whatever you call it?'

'Yes, and of course there's the house he bought her.'

'Who has the deeds?'

'Catherine.'

'But you don't know if she has any money left?'

'No. We're close, but I've never thought to ask. Anyway, who could she owe money to?'

'Anyone, although I rather doubt it's her hat maker. Her coke dealer maybe, or her bookie, if she's into that. Or a rough boy friend looking for an easy few quid. I gather she's had a few of those. The question is, who would she owe enough money to for them to threaten her that heavily? Or maybe she doesn't owe anyone any money and it's something else.'

'Like what?'

I shrugged again. 'Perhaps we'd better ask her.'

'Do you want me to?'

I thought about it for a moment. 'No,' I said. 'She might not tell you the truth. Mind you, she might not tell me the truth either. You realise this changes the nature of the job.'

'Does that worry you?' Elizabeth asked.

'I might collect the next motor aimed at your sister, and, yes, that does worry me.'

'I'll double your fee.'

I had to smile. 'It's not the money that worries me, it's if I want to put my life on the line.'

'And do you?'

'I promised her I would protect her last night, and I keep my promises.'

'Thank you, Mr Sharman.'

'You can call me Nick if you want.'

She blushed. 'Thank you, but only when we're alone,' she said. People are weird.

'Sure,' I said.

'I don't want you to leave her side.'

'Listen, Miss Pike – '

'Elizabeth.'

'When we're alone.'

She nodded.

'Elizabeth,' I went on. 'Catherine is kind of independent. She had to be, with her upbringing, or lack of it. She told me a bit about that last night too,' I said before she could interrupt me. 'She's scared, but "never leave her side", I doubt that. I'll do my best, but that's the most I can promise.'

'Do what you can.'

'I will. So what's the plan for today?'

'I'm going into the office and Catherine wants to do some shopping. Stick to her like glue.'

'Even in the changing room.'

'Don't be funny.'

'Does she pay, by the way? Or busk it, like you?' I couldn't resist it.

Elizabeth blushed again, a real cherry. 'I'd rather you didn't mention that, if you don't mind. That was before Daddy died. Things have changed. I don't do that now.'

'I'll keep that our little secret,' I said.

'Good.' She abandoned the toast, pushed back her chair and made for the door. She looked at her watch. It was eight fifty.

'Will you wait here for Catherine, and then go along with what she wants to do for the rest of the day?'

I nodded and lit a cigarette. After another cup of coffee my hangover slowly started to subside but I still wasn't ready for food.

The next half-hour was an interesting lesson in how the other half lives. I was offered breakfast at least three times by Miranda and Courtneidge who popped in and out with trays of food that no one was there to eat. I asked Miranda what was up, and she told me that it was the custom of the household to lay out a huge breakfast however many of the family were at home. I asked what happened to the leftovers and she told me they went into the bin. Jesus, I though, conspicuous consumption.

The next time she came in with more coffee I asked her where the rest of the family was. She told me that Mr David had gone to the office and his wife never ate breakfast and Mr Simon took his in bed.

Catherine came down at nine thirty. She was wearing very baggy blue jeans rolled high above the ankle, a short red T-shirt that exposed an inch or two of smooth skin above the waistband of the trousers, and black spike-heeled shoes over red socks. She apologised nicely for her lateness. She seemed fully recovered from the previous evening and piled a plate high with enough fry-up to satisfy a navvy. 'Hungry?' I asked.

'Ravenous. You?'

'No, I've got a bit of a hangover.'

'Never get them myself,' she said. 'I've always thought they were overrated.'

'If you never get them, how do you know?' I asked as I looked at the food.

She shrugged and bit into a piece of kidney. I shuddered and poured more coffee.

'I don't know how to say this,' she said after she chewed and swallowed the food. 'But I owe you one for last night.'

'Don't mention it.'

'But someone tried to run me down.'

'Not necessarily.'

'But that car nearly hit me, you saw it.'

'I also saw a bloke holding a gun on the way in, except it wasn't a gun, was it? It was a Nikon 35mm with a pistol grip and I could have killed the poor bastard on the strength of it.'

'I'm sorry. I'm being a bit of a nuisance, aren't I?'

'I'm getting well paid,' I said.

'Money isn't everything.' Only fuckers with loads ever say that.

I changed the subject. 'Elizabeth is very worried about you.'

'I know.'

'She wants me to guard your body from here on in. I told her what you told me last night about the telephone calls you've been getting.'

'I wish you hadn't.'

'I had to. We both want to know who's threatening you.'

'I have no idea.'

'Are you sure?'

'Of course.'

'Think about it.'

'Did you agree to be my bodyguard?' she asked, evading the question.

'I'm here, aren't I?'

'Thank God, I'm so pleased. Have you got a gun?'

'Yes.'

'Can I see it?'

'Why?'

'Because I want to.'

'You're the boss.' I took the Baby B from its ankle holster and held it up to show her. She got up to get a better view. She ran her fingers along the short blue barrel and looked at me through hooded eyelids. I swear to God it turned me on, hangover or no hangover.

When she spoke her voice was husky. 'Would you use it?' For a minute I didn't know if she was referring to the gun or what.

'As a last resort,' I said.

We stood there in silence for a moment. 'I thought we were going shopping.' I put the gun away.

She snapped out of it. 'Yes, we are,' she said and the moment had gone.

I hate shopping. My spree the previous day had been done on

my toes and took forty minutes max. I just knew that Catherine was a serious shopper.

And so she was, a real pro. We shopped all the way from Covent Garden to Knightsbridge, touching base in Bond Street and St Christopher's Place. She shopped with manic intensity and pretty soon the boot of the Rolls was full and parcels were intruding onto the back seat.

I trailed after her like a pet poodle. Yes, I carried some bags but I kept an eye out to see if we were followed and I saw no one.

'I haven't been shopping since my father died,' she said as we stopped for Bloody Marys at the Connaught. 'You must be good for me.' And she touched my cheek with her fingertip.

I won't say that I didn't like it, because I did.

We lunched in Beauchamp Place and had tea at the Savoy. We got back to Curzon Street around five and I went off to soak my weary feet in the bath.

'Dinner's at eight,' she told me as we parted at her door. 'Be there or be square.'

'I'll be there,' I said.

8

Dinner was an unforgettable experience, as were most of the meals I took at Curzon Street. But this one was the worst. I crawled out of the bath about six fifteen and wandered about the room in clean boxers for a while, smoking and sipping at a beer. I was sitting on the bed and running the previous two days' events through my mind when the telephone on the bedside table rang. It was Elizabeth on the internal line inviting me to meet the family in the drawing room at seven for drinks. Another bloody room with a title of its own, I thought.

I changed into a new, navy blue suit, pale shirt and patterned tie. It took me some time to find the drawing room but I eventually heard the sound of conversation from behind a closed door on the ground floor. I pushed the door open and rolled in feeling as sharp as a new razor blade. The three people on the other side were togged up like they were off to a night at the opera. I felt as under-dressed as a lettuce leaf that had missed the oil and vinegar boat.

The three, two men and a woman, were all strangers to me; neither Elizabeth nor Catherine were anywhere to be seen.

'Sorry,' I said, standing at the doorway. 'But the invitation said "come as you are".'

Three pairs of eyes swung towards me and I gave the owners the benefit of my teeth in a big, disarming grin.

'How fortunate you weren't in the shower when it arrived,' said a tall, willowy fellow in a white tux and black tie, who was half folded up against the mantelpiece of the dead fireplace. He held a cigarette languidly in one hand; a half-full cocktail glass was tilted in the other. His hair was dirty blond and a fringe flopped in an untidy comma over one eye. I knew at once we were going to be bosom pals before the night was out.

'I almost was,' I said.

'That might have made life a little more interesting,' remarked the woman in a low-cut black evening gown, who was sitting in an over-stuffed armchair. Her bodice was a little over-stuffed too and looked in danger of surrendering to gravity at any moment. Her expression was bored and miserable and although she wasn't bad looking, her face had already begun to set into middle-aged crossness that I guessed would be her expression for the rest of her life.

I kept the grin on until it felt as if it might turn round and bite me.

Elizabeth saved the day by walking through the open french doors and coming to my rescue. 'Mr Sharman,' she said, 'forgive me for not being here to greet you, and most of all for not telling you about our habit of dressing for dinner. It completely slipped my mind that you might not have a dinner jacket with you.'

I made a mental note always to carry one with me in future, possibly in a holster strapped to my other ankle.

'If you give Courtneidge your size,' she continued, 'I'll have one sent around tomorrow.' She made it sound as casual as ordering an extra pint of milk. 'I think Mr Sharman is wearing a very nice suit,' said the blond man holding up the chimney breast. 'Although possibly his tie is just a little chi-chi for evening wear.'

I felt like hooking him onto the picture rail. Elizabeth stopped me with a cool hand. 'Pay no attention to Simon,' she said. 'He always has had leanings towards comedy, but his attempts don't always come off.'

I said nothing, just let her keep her hand where it was on mine. I liked it.

'Now let me introduce you to everyone. Simon Pike is my late father's nephew. He's staying here until his own house is ready for occupation.'

I nodded to the comic but made no attempt to shake hands. For his part, he didn't even nod in response.

'Unfortunately it's taking rather longer than he expected,' said the woman in the chair. 'And a brief visit is slowly turning into a marathon stay.'

Simon shot the woman a withering look.

'This is Claire,' said Elizabeth. 'My brother David's wife.'

Claire raised her hand and I walked over and took it. It was chubby, with fat little fingers made even thicker by jewelled rings. I squeezed it gently and gave it back intact. 'How do you do?' I said like a good little boy at his first grown-up party, which is just about how I felt.

Claire gave me an impersonation of a smile and told me how delighted she was to meet me, which is not at all how she looked.

The other man in the room stepped between us and stuck out his hand. 'David Pike,' he said. 'How do you do, Mr Sharman?'

'I'm fine. How was the US trip?' I asked.

'Exhausting, but it accomplished what was necessary. At this moment I'd rather talk about why Lizzy thinks we need an in-house private detective.'

'I have my reasons,' said Elizabeth. 'Private reasons, and it's as much my house as yours.'

'At the moment,' said David.

I was left holding his hand while this short altercation took place. It was dry and strong and its grip was more than firm.

After he released my aching fingers the whole family stood back and gave me the once-over. I felt like shuffling my feet and saying something like 'Gee shucks'. I was suffering from aristocracy awe and I didn't like it one bit. I thought back to my days in the job and tried to get my mind right.

'Miss Pike feels that a little security on the premises at this time wouldn't go amiss,' I said. 'The arrangement is between us and –'

Simon didn't let me finish. 'For however much you can screw out of her for a wild goose chase.'

Elizabeth butted in before I could speak. 'Mr Sharman is charging his usual rate,' she said. 'Not a penny more.'

'Then he must be more stupid than he looks, or else it's your body he's after,' said Simon.

That one went closer to the target than I liked and I was halfway to the fireplace and ready to give Simon a right-hander when Elizabeth caught my arm again. 'No,' she said.

Simon hadn't even flinched. He must have been tougher than he looked or else someone had always been around to fight his battles for him. I suspected the latter.

I stopped and felt like a berk. 'I think you should apologise to Miss Pike,' I said. It sounded a bit weak, even to me.

Simon sniggered.

'Simon,' David intervened. 'You are in my father's house, behave yourself.'

Simon shrugged. 'Sorry, love,' he said sarcastically to Elizabeth.

I felt as if he'd got the better of me and I didn't like that one bit.

Elizabeth defused the situation by offering me a drink. She poured me a vodka rocks from the side table that groaned under its load of bottles of booze. The drink was freezing cold and tasted good on my parched lips. 'If that chump makes any more cracks like that I'm going to punch his lights out,' I said quietly.

'Ignore him,' she replied.

At that point Catherine blew into the room wearing a black lace creation that left so little to the imagination that it almost made an imagination redundant. In her hair was plaited a fresh gardenia.

'Good evening,' she said, as we all stood pop-eyed at her entrance. 'Do you like my new frock?'

'I'm sure it will be splendid when it's finished,' said Claire.

Catherine went to the drinks table and poured three inches of vodka over an iceberg of cubes and a small slice of lemon, and showed it the tonic bottle. She'd told me her mother was a piss artist. Like mother, like daughter obviously. 'Oh Claire,' she said. 'You've always got your finger on the pulse of chic. How I wish I'd taken you shopping with me today.'

I could see the old claws were coming out with a vengeance.

Catherine picked up her drink and made directly for me. She crooked her arm into mine. 'Fat old bitch,' she said, just loud enough for me to hear. 'She gets all her outfits from C & A.'

'Catherine,' said Simon, 'if you will insist in fraternising with the staff, at least be kind enough to let us all in on the conversation. It's so rude to whisper.'

I stiffened but Catherine just smiled. 'Simon,' she said smoothly, 'I didn't see you lurking there in the corner. You really should have taken those self-assertion classes I was telling you about.'

He flushed slightly and was just about to make another snide remark, which I'm sure would have left me no option but to deck him, when a maid who wasn't Miranda so who must have been Constance appeared at the door and informed us that dinner was served.

We de-camped and strolled to the dining room. It was the size of a rugby pitch and looked out over Curzon Street. The dining table was a desert of white linen set with gleaming silver cutlery.

I've enjoyed more sociable meals. For a start, we were seated as far away from each other as was possible, which given the personality of certain members of the family wasn't a bad idea. Then what with all the fancy silver decorations and flowers and crystal shit that were piled up across the centre of the table, it was difficult to believe that you were doing anything but eating alone. Courtneidge and Constance served the meal.

We ate cold salmon and salad followed by strawberries and cream. It was hardly worth getting all dressed up for. But what did I know? For the previous few months I'd eaten most of my meals out of a tin or between two slices of bread over the kitchen sink to save on the washing up.

We got to the coffee and port stage of the meal with hardly any conversation. But when the cigars came out, the claws came out again with them. I was sitting next to Claire who was placed opposite Catherine, and Simon sat opposite me. We were closest to the foot of the table – which still looked about a mile away – at which Elizabeth was seated. David sat at the head of the table.

Courtneidge left the pot of coffee on the sideboard. The port bottle was moving round the table. I half expected the ladies to leave us but the three of them stayed in their seats as if superglued.

Simon was the first to speak after the two servants had left and Courtneidge had closed the double doors behind them.

'So how was the launch of your new magazine?' he asked.

'Excellent,' said Elizabeth.

'I saw you in the papers this morning. It's a pity I wasn't invited.'

'Would you have gone?' she asked.

'Of course,' replied Simon. 'Anything for a free drink.'

'Except it wouldn't have been free. Pike Publications were paying for it.'

'It would have been free to me,' said Simon cattily. 'I don't have any holdings in the company, as you well know.'

'Which is why you weren't invited,' piped up Catherine.

'You bitch.'

'Steady,' I said.

Simon turned his venom onto me. 'Oh, the knight in shining armour has woken up. Only it's rather tarnished these days, so I've heard.'

'Oh, do be quiet, Simon,' said David. 'You can be such a crashing bore at times. You know we have important things to talk about.'

'Yes, but I didn't realise we were going to talk in front of the hired help,' said Simon.

I glanced over at Elizabeth and saw the pleading look in her eyes. I didn't take the bait. Simon looked well pissed off and I knew I'd done the right thing.

'Simon, I shan't tell you again,' said David. 'Mr Sharman is Elizabeth's guest, and I insist that you treat him as such.'

'A guest!' spat Simon, but that was all.

'I'm sorry, Mr Sharman,' David said to me. 'Now where were we? Oh, yes. Tomorrow, my father's will is going to be read. We are to gather at the solicitors' at ten. I imagine we will all go together with Vincent in the Rolls. Is that satisfactory?'

'I want Mr Sharman to come,' said Elizabeth.

It was news to me.

'Whatever for?' asked David.

'Because I do.'

'I'm sorry, Elizabeth, but I really can't allow Mr Sharman to be present.'

'But I want him there.'

'Why?'

I watched the exchange like a game of tennis with the words being batted back and forth across the white tablecloth.

'Hey,' I said. 'Slow down. If you want to talk about me, perhaps I'd better leave.'

'Stay where you are,' ordered Elizabeth.

'Yes, ma'am,' I said.

'My dear Elizabeth,' said David with the kind of exaggerated patience you save for fools and children, 'is it really necessary?' He looked at me. 'And forgive me, Mr Sharman, for talking about you as if you weren't here. Is it really necessary for Mr Sharman to be present at the reading of the will?'

'It really isn't,' I said.

'It is if I say it is,' responded Elizabeth stubbornly.

'I could just come along and wait outside,' I offered. I really didn't know what all the fuss was about. I was damn sure I wasn't a beneficiary.

'That sounds like a fine compromise,' said David. 'Elizabeth, is that all right with you?'

'I suppose so,' she said icily. 'But I don't know why you should always have the last word on everything.'

There was a lot of shit going on under the surface of that room and I didn't particularly want to be around when it floated to the surface and stank the place out.

'Because he thinks he's going to get lucky in the will tomorrow and end up king of the castle,' Simon said nastily.

'Why don't you be quiet, Simon,' snapped Catherine. 'You really do have appalling manners. Perhaps Mr Sharman could teach you a few.'

'When I need lessons in manners from him or an Australian bastard, I'll ask for them, thank you.'

That did it. I got ready to do a leaper over the table and knock some manners into him.

'Nick, don't,' Elizabeth begged.

'So it's Nick, is it?' put in Claire. 'How cosy.'

'Shut up, Claire,' shouted Elizabeth. 'I can't stand any more of this.' She jumped up from her seat, knocking her port across the white damask where it pooled like fresh blood. She threw her napkin into the pool and fled the room.

I pushed my own seat back and followed her. As I went I said to Simon, 'You've been lucky so far, pal, but your luck's running out.' He toasted me with his port glass and I gave him what I hoped was a killing glare. I might as well have sent him a begging letter.

I chased Elizabeth through corridors and hallways with

polished wood floors and panelled walls that amplified our footsteps like gunfire. I caught up with her on a staircase hung with old masters which I wouldn't have given to a dog to look at. I held her by the arm and pulled her round to face me. She was crying and her mascara had run into black lines down her face. She brushed the lines into streaks and leant against the wall, sobbing bitterly.

'What was all that about?' I asked.

'Oh Nick,' she said, through her tears. 'I do so want to keep the family together, but I feel like I'm banging my head against a brick wall.'

'Maybe you're trying too hard.'

'At least tomorrow when the will's been read we'll know what's happening.'

'There seems to be enough to go round. Why worry?'

'Because it was Daddy's company, and his life, and now he's gone. I want to see it get bigger and better. I miss him so much. And now you tell me that Catherine, my one true friend, is in danger.

'Elizabeth,' I said, 'don't get hysterical.'

But she was. Her hands had fisted and she was waving them all over the shop. I hate all that shit, always have. I didn't want to slap her like in the films, so instead I avoided her flying fists and moved in and held her tightly. She was as stiff as one of the canvases on the wall. I could feel her heart beating.

'Stop it,' I said and she gave one last desperate sob and grabbed at me. Her body arched and all the pain in the world was in her voice as she tried to speak. 'Relax,' I said. 'Just let it all out.'

She did, all down the front of my new suit. There must have been a gallon of grief inside her and my new wool worsted soaked it all up. I held her and rocked her and slowly she calmed down. Finally I let her go and she stepped back. She was out of breath and her make-up was a ruin.

She saw me looking and said, 'I must look awful.'

I could have written the script.

'You look great,' I said, and she did.

'I've never cried before, not properly. Not since Daddy died. Just little weeps. I feel better for that. Thanks, Nick.'

'A pleasure.'

'I ruined your suit.'

I looked down and she was right. 'Forget it.'

'I'll buy you a new one.'

Why do rich people always have to spoil things? I can never get over it.

'Never mind,' I said.

'Have I said something wrong?'

'No,' I replied, and she hadn't. Not by her standards. She just had too much money.

She didn't look convinced. 'Are you sure?'

I smiled – why shouldn't I? I'd just held a very beautiful woman very close and it had felt good.

'I promise,' I said. 'I'm glad to be a help.'

'I'll be better with you around.'

I felt about ten feet tall. 'Good,' I said.

'I'm going to my room now.' She smiled. 'I'm going to take a bath and have an early night. I hate to desert you, but I feel exhausted, and I must get my beauty sleep.'

'I can't think of anyone who needs it less,' I said.

'You're so gallant, Mr Sharman.'

'I'm a bit out of it myself. I think I'll turn in early too.' It was true, I was cream crackered.

'Take a look around,' she urged. 'And treat the place as your own. Everyone else does.' She added the last three words bitterly.

'I will,' I said. 'Just take it easy. I'll sort everything out.'

'I only hope you can.'

'Don't worry.'

'I'll organise a dinner jacket for you in the morning. I'm so sorry about that. I didn't mean to make you look a fool.'

'Don't worry. It's hardly the biggest social gaffe I've ever made.'

'Let's meet for breakfast and we'll talk then,' she suggested.

'I'll look forward to it.'

'Good night then.'

'Good night, Elizabeth.'

I thought she was going to say more and I wanted her to. But she just blew me a kiss and walked up the stairs into the shadows, vanishing like a wraith.

9

I didn't go back to the remnants of dinner, instead I made my way back to my suite and switched on the TV in the sitting room and made myself a vodka and tonic. I looked out of the french windows and lit a cigarette. The air outside was heavy and dusty and there was no trace of a breeze. I didn't bother putting on any lights but just allowed the TV screen to illuminate the room with its flickering colours as darkness came.

Finally, when it was fully dark, I switched on a small table lamp and looked at the pile of butts in the ashtray. I threw two empty tonic bottles into the wastepaper basket and decided to hit the sack. I pulled myself off the sofa, feeling old and weary. There was a tap on the door. I went over and opened it. Catherine was leaning against the door frame with a bottle of champagne in each hand. 'Hi, Nick,' she said. 'I thought you'd run out on me.'

'No,' I replied. 'I just wasn't crazy about the company you were keeping.'

'You wanna know a secret? Neither was I. So I liberated two bottles of the best shampoo that Pike money can buy and here I am. Can I come in?'

I stepped back into the room. 'Of course. You're welcome.'

'Thanks.'

'There should be some glasses.'

'If there isn't, this is not part of the Pike empire.'

I found two flutes in the glass collection on top of the fridge. Catherine eased the cork off one of the bottles with an ease born of practice. She filled both glasses and we touched rims. 'To crime,' she said.

'And punishment,' I replied.

She sat on the sofa and the skirt of her dress slid up her thighs. I averted my eyes and offered her a cigarette. 'Thank you.' As she leaned forward to accept a light I could just about see her navel. If she was trying to get me at it, she was succeeding admirably.

'Can we have some music?' she asked.

'There isn't any.'

'Of course there is.' She came out of the depths of the sofa like a cat and went over to the bookcase. She fiddled around and a section slid open. Inside was a cute little stereo system. She switched it on and found an FM stereo station playing jazz standards without the benefit of some jerk of a DJ. She adjusted the volume so that Anita O'Day oozed out of the concealed speakers like syrup off a warm pancake.

'Amazing,' I said.

'Didn't Miranda tell you about this when she showed you your rooms? I'll have words with her in the morning.'

'Don't do that,' I said. 'I think my private eye charisma was blinding her when she showed me up.'

'I'm not surprised,' said Catherine. 'It's been doing the same to me.' She dimpled prettily and I dimpled prettily back. At least I think I did.

Anita O'Day was replaced by Ray Charles doing *One Mint Julep* and Catherine said, 'Wanna dance?'

'Sure.' She came into my arms and tucked her head into my neck and I smelt the freshness of her. Her body fitted mine down to the finest detail.

We danced to Ray Charles, then Ella singing *Where or When*, then Sinatra's version of *Love for Sale*, until Jimmy Smith pounded out *Hobo Flats* which defeated us both and we collapsed onto the sofa.

'That was nice,' she said.

'It was, it's been a while.'

'A while what?'

'Since I danced with anyone.'

'I don't believe that.' She topped up our glasses and lit a cigarette.

Suddenly she leant over and kissed me on the side of the mouth. She tasted of tobacco and alcohol and her lips were as soft and slippery as melted butter.

'Are you trying to seduce me?' I asked.

'Could be, but it's not me you want, is it?'

'What?'

'It's Elizabeth, isn't it?'

'Shit, Catherine.'

'We could just have a fuck and leave it at that,' she said.

'I don't think it's good practice to sleep with the clients.'

She thought about it for a moment. 'But I'm not really your client, Elizabeth is.'

'You're close enough for comfort, and you're splitting hairs.'

'How about getting smashed with the client?'

'I'm always up for that.'

She stood up and opened the other bottle of champagne. 'Let's do it then.'

And we did.

God knows what time we finished drinking, but I do know that we got through every drop of booze in the room before Catherine went unsteadily back to her rooms through the connecting door to my suite.

I left the mess and the light on, and went to bed leaving a trail of clothes behind me. I tossed and turned for a few hours. I finally came to about seven thirty and lay there fighting back the urge to vomit. Bad news, Nick, I thought. Throwing up in the morning is serious bodily abuse. What was wrong with me? Getting old was the only answer I could come up with. Getting old and cold and past it. I put the thought away as gently as I would have placed a precious stone on a velvet mount.

I crawled out of bed and thanked Christ for the slight breeze puffing the white curtains at the window. I stood for a while in the relief it gave from the heat of the sun that was already trying to melt the brickwork. Then I braved the shaving mirror.

I scraped stubble and skin from my face. I thought that if it had belonged to a friend I would have sat down and given him a serious talking to about an excessive life style. I tamed my hair with cold water and beat it to submission with a comb from my case. At first it fought back but I soon showed it who was boss.

I dressed in jeans, black loafers with red socks and a black polo shirt. I picked up a pair of tortoiseshell Mulberry shades from the dresser and hung them on my nose and then I gave up. What the hell, I was as ready as I was ever going to be to face the morning.

I went to the breakfast room. Elizabeth was sitting at the table alone, cutting a slice of toast into matchsticks and dipping them into a cup of coffee.

'Jesus,' I said. 'What's that, occupational therapy?'

She was wearing another black suit and all the accessories. She looked good enough to eat, except I had no appetite.

'You could say that,' she replied. 'What's up with you? You look awful.'

'Thanks,' I said. 'You're making me feel much better. I'm the victim of a recurring hangover. Two days running. I'm never at my best with doors banging inside my head.'

'You shouldn't drink so much.'

I had heard that before. I sat down opposite her with my cup and saucer rattling in my unsteady grip. 'Thanks for the advice, but I'm only trying to keep Catherine company.'

'That wasn't what you were hired for.'

'That seems to be precisely what I was hired for.'

'Have it your own way.'

'Sorry,' I said. 'I'll go out and come in again if you like, and we can start over fresh.'

'Why bother?'

'Why bother to do anything?'

'I thought you wanted to be bothered to help us?'

'I do, I do. Just give me a few minutes.'

We sat in a silence that was almost palpable. I drank my coffee and she filled hers with soggy crumbs that made me feel quite nauseous again.

'Elizabeth.'

'Yes?'

'Stop doing that.'

'What?'

'Playing with your food.'

'I'm so sorry.' She pushed the cup away so that the liquid slopped into the saucer. I finished my coffee and took a wrinkled pack of cigarettes from my back pocket. I lit one from a book of matches and offered the pack to Elizabeth. She took the cigarette from my mouth so I lit another.

'I apologize,' I said. 'I'm not much good at conversation in the morning.'

'I'll remember that,' she said through a mouthful of grey-blue smoke.

I gave her half a smile and she gave me back the other half.

'So let's get down to business,' I said. 'What time does this show get on the road?'

'We're due at the solicitors' at ten, so I suppose we'll leave here at about nine fifteen.' I looked at my watch. Eight fifteen. 'The rest should be down for breakfast soon,' she went on.

'You're sure you want me to come?'

'Of course.'

'I'll leave you to it then. I think I'd better change into something more befitting a trip to the lawyers. Have you spoken to Catherine about those phone calls?'

Elizabeth nodded. 'She wasn't too happy that you told me. But yes, we have talked about them.'

'No fresh ideas?'

'No.'

'We'd better all talk as soon as possible.'

'Very well. But let's get this will business out of the way first.'

'You're the boss,' I said. 'I'll see you later.' I left her to the remains of her breakfast and went upstairs and stood under a cold shower until my head was numb. I dressed in a suit and tie. I got back downstairs in time to meet the rest of the family in the hall. They were all dressed in variations of funeral clothes and I was glad I'd changed.

I travelled in the front of the Rolls with Vincent, who didn't say one word to me for the whole journey. The five family members squeezed into the back, so I probably got the best of the deal. The family lawyer was in Lincoln's Inn and the drive took twenty-five minutes or so. Vincent parked right outside on a double yellow line.

I followed the family into the lawyers' office, which was a converted town house that smelled of beeswax, fresh flowers and cigar smoke. We went into a waiting room and after a minute or so a woman in a dark suit, with a respectful, troubled look that she probably thought befitted the occasion, came in and led the others through a set of double doors opposite. I stayed behind and sat in a leather Chesterfield chair.

I sat and smoked and drank a cup of coffee that an amazingly attractive receptionist with breasts that fought at the confines of her white blouse brought me. Halfway through the second cigarette one of the double doors burst open and banged against the wall. David flew through the doorway and down the hall shouting, 'I'm not staying a moment more. Claire, come on, we'll get a cab.'

Claire wobbled after him and Simon followed her. Elizabeth

came to the doorway, looked after them and said something I didn't catch. Then she came across to the waiting room.

'What the hell was all that about?' I asked.

'The bloody will, of course. Daddy left everything equally to all his children, including Catherine. David wasn't keen on the idea. He's off to his own solicitors to contest the will.'

'Christ,' I said. 'The poop's hit the propeller.'

'Very apt, Mr Sharman, very apt indeed. Shall we go?'

'How's Catherine taken all this?' I asked.

'She's not happy. She's in there crying.'

'And I'm fresh out of clean hankies,' I said.

She ignored the remark and went back over to the office. I stubbed out my cigarette and waited. After a minute or so, Elizabeth and Catherine appeared in the doorway with an old boy behind them. He was nervously dry-washing his hands and talking to them in a low tone so that I couldn't hear him. Catherine came over to me. Her eyes were full of tears and she leant up against me as Elizabeth said her farewells. The old boy retreated into his office and shut the door.

'What's the plan?' I asked.

'I don't know,' said Elizabeth.

'I could fancy a drink.'

'Not the most unusual state of affairs,' she replied, and walked down the corridor away from me.

'Maybe not,' I said to her retreating back.

We had Vincent stop at the Inn On The Park and trooped into the cocktail bar. It was early and just a couple of sports were taking the water. I ordered three large bourbons, straight up, from the bar. It was that kind of morning. Then I joined the two women at a table in a lonely corner of the room.

The waiter pranced over with our order and pranced off again. 'I should get his number for Leee,' I said.

'Must you always make jokes?' asked Elizabeth.

'Sorry,' I said. 'Just trying to lighten the load.'

Catherine smiled for the first time since we'd left the lawyers' office. 'Leave him, Liz. He's probably right. Leee would love that boy.'

'So what's cooking?' I asked through the smoky aftertaste of my drink.

'What's cooking is the estate's in flux,' said Elizabeth.

The estate's in a state, I thought, but didn't vocalise it. 'How long for?' I asked no one.

'How the hell do I know?' Elizabeth snapped.

'It's all my fault,' said Catherine. 'I had no idea.'

'It's not your fault,' Elizabeth told her, 'it's David's.'

'And Daddy's,' said Catherine.

'The money was his to do with as he wanted.' Elizabeth picked up her drink. 'If he wanted to leave you a third of it, fine by me. Christ Almighty, there's enough for three thousand people, let alone three.'

That was almost what I'd said to her the previous evening. 'But David didn't see it that way?' I asked.

'He's a bloody pig,' said Elizabeth. 'Just like the rest of them.'

'What are you going to do?'

'Do?' said Elizabeth. 'Do? We're going to have a party, that's what we're going to do.'

'When?' Catherine seemed surprised.

'Tonight,' said Elizabeth. She finished her drink with a swallow and stood up, picked up her bag and marched out. Catherine and I looked at each other and followed her to the door.

Vincent was patiently waiting in the car. He whisked us round the corner, back to the house. The three of us went into the conservatory and Miranda was summoned to serve us more booze. She made a jug of martinis, large enough to drown a donkey, and left us to it.

'Do you think a party is a good idea?' I asked.

'Why not?' said Elizabeth. 'I'm going to show David whose side I'm on.'

'And a party's the way to do that?'

'As good a way as any. I want him to know that I support Catherine all the way.'

Catherine smiled her gratitude round the edge of her martini glass.

'Have you had any more threatening calls?' I asked Catherine.

'Not since you arrived,' she said.

'I'd love to think it was my influence, but I doubt it,' I said. 'And I don't know about inviting a bunch of people here. If someone is out to get you, it would be a great opportunity. I'm on my tod, and this is a big house with lots of nooks and crannies. With the best will in the world, I can't be with you every second.'

'Do you think that one of our friends is behind this?' asked Catherine. 'Because it will be our friends who are coming tonight.'

'Who knows?' I said. 'But at this short notice, there will be no formal invites. Anyone could get into the house. It's got more entrances than Harrod's and in this weather they'll all be open wide.'

'The servants will be here.'

'They're hardly security experts.'

'What do you think, Catherine?' asked Elizabeth.

'I think we should have a party.'

'So do I,' said Elizabeth. 'And if we're going to have one, I've got a million and one things to do. I've got to invite some people, do some shopping and brief the staff. I'd better get moving.'

'Me too,' said Catherine. 'I'm so glad I went shopping yesterday. I'm going upstairs to get on the phone. I'll invite everyone I can think of, Liz. I know who you want here. Leave it to me, you get out to the shops. I'll take care of everything. How many should we cater for? Sixty?'

'That sounds about right. I'll get Courtneidge to tell David and Claire and Simon. Do you think they'll come?'

'Who knows?' shrugged Catherine. 'Nick, you can come upstairs and keep me company?'

'Okay,' I said and we dumped our empty glasses and left the room.

I accompanied Catherine upstairs in the lift and followed her into her suite. The shape of the rooms was the same as mine, but reversed. The furniture was covered in a pale brocade which matched the curtains covering the french windows. They opened onto a tiny balcony that was the twin of the one outside my sitting room.

She put a Cowboy Junkies CD onto the player at a whisper and sat down in an armchair next to a table which supported a telephone and a leather address book. I found an ashtray and a pile of magazines and sat on the sofa. First she called Courtneidge and put him in the picture, and then she called Leee, told him about the party, and asked him to drop by at four, so that he could do her hair and then stick around for the festivities. Then she got down to the serious telephoning and I sat with my eyes closed and half listened as she invited twenty or so friends to crack a bottle of vino later.

Lunch was served by Constance at one thirty. She appeared and disappeared like a puff of smoke, leaving a trolley groaning with goodies.

I picked at a Waldorf salad and drank some sparkling wine while we watched *Neighbours*. Gee, but it's great to be rich. After lunch we played Trivial Pursuit and I beat Catherine two games to one. We drank more wine and Catherine made more phone calls. At three thirty she went for a bath. I took my glass and a fresh bottle out onto the balcony and stood in the sun, looking out over the roof tops and down at the conservatory and paved garden beneath me. At four o'clock precisely the internal telephone rang. I answered it. Constance told me that Mr Leee was at the front door. I asked her to send him up.

Two minutes later he blew in like a mini typhoon and he gave me a hug, accepted a drink, stole a cigarette, complained about the heat, getting cabs in the West End, the weight of his handbag and asked where Catherine was, all in one twenty-second burst of energy.

'Slow down, Leee,' I said. 'You're making me feel quite weary.'

'I've got just the thing, dear.' He produced a wrap from the pocket of his white jacket and cut out two fat lines on a small mirror before you could say knife, or razor blade. 'Give this a go, it's good stuff,' he said, and produced a thick straw cut down to about three inches long. He snarfed his line and danced around the room for a moment, then changed the CD from Elgar's *Variations* to *Guns 'n' Roses* and whacked the volume up high. 'Let's get into a party mood,' he shouted above the music.

I was game. I snorted my line, cleaned the mirror with my forefinger and gave my gums a treat.

Catherine poked her head round the bedroom door. I could just see that she was wrapped in a bath towel. 'I might have guessed you were here.'

'Aphrodite fresh from the pool,' said Lee. I thought he was getting a bit mixed up but I was too stoned to care.

'I'll just get something on and be right with you,' Catherine told him.

'Don't bother on our account, dear,' said Leee. *'Au naturelle* will suit, I'm sure.'

Catherine grinned. 'What are you on, Leee?'

'Wouldn't you like to know.'

'Don't corrupt Mr Sharman.'

'He's past corruption, dear, just take a look at his face. And by the way, why isn't he collating or whatever it is that he's supposed to do? I get the feeling he wasn't telling me the whole truth the other night.'

'It's my day off,' I said before Catherine could speak.

'Of course it is, dear.' He looked over at Catherine and pulled a face. 'Of course it is.'

It was a good afternoon. The kind that arrives unbidden every now and then. I lit a cigarette and opened another bottle of wine from the ice bucket.

Catherine came back into the room in a long, thin silken robe that managed to hide everything and nothing at the same time. Leee raised his eyebrows and sat her in an upright chair. He pulled out his bag of scissors and combs and went to work on her hair. He teased and played with it for half an hour until he pronounced himself satisfied with the results. It still looked like it hadn't been touched for a month and I told him so.

'But that's the idea,' he said. 'Silly boy. It's wild, it's free, it's so ... ' He was lost for words.

'Leee,' I said drily.

'Exactly.' He smiled happily. 'Or are you teasing me? It doesn't matter if you are. I'm happy and so is dear Catherine, aren't you?'

'I am,' said Catherine admiring herself in Leee's hand mirror.

'Now how about you, Nick?' Leee held his comb aloft. 'Can I do something for you?'

'I don't think so. I couldn't stand the attention it would bring me.'

'You are teasing,' he said.

As the day became evening, the volume of the music dropped and we listened to some Steve Earle and Randy Travis. Leee opened up about his fantasy of being a cowboy singer and rolled a joint. We got slightly higher and Catherine ordered roast beef sandwiches and beer for dinner.

'There'll be lots of food at the party,' she said. 'And I don't want Cook throwing a moody.'

'What about Elizabeth and the rest?'

'She's going to join us in a minute. The rest can go and screw themselves.'

'That's the spirit, dear,' said Leee.

Courtneidge appeared with the food at seven and Elizabeth came in behind him with a pile of parcels. 'This lot's for you,' she said to me.

'What is it?'

'Open them and see,' said Leee. 'I love surprises.'

I emptied the boxes and bags and found a double-breasted dinner jacket and matching trousers with a thin satin stripe up the sides of the legs, three white dress shirts, six pairs of silk socks, a bow tie, and a pair of black patent leather pumps.

'Thank you,' I said.

'Miranda got your sizes,' Elizabeth explained. 'I hope they fit. And Catherine and I thought you could use these.' She dug into her handbag and brought out a small, gift-wrapped parcel. She handed it to me. I peeled off the wrapping paper and found a leather box. I opened the box. Nestling on a satin inlay were a pair of cufflinks identical to the ones that she had put into her pocket in the shop in Molton Street so many weeks before.

'Don't worry, they're paid for,' she said and the two women collapsed into a fit of giggles.

'What's the joke?' asked Leee. But we refused to enlighten him and he soon forgot about it.

'You must try everything on as soon as we've eaten.' Leee grinned. 'You can change here if you like.'

'I'll do it next door,' I said.

'You're so modest, I love it.'

We sat down to eat. 'What are you wearing tonight, Leee? One of those?' I pointed to the DJ.

He looked at Catherine and they grinned conspiratorially. 'Oh no, dear,' he said. 'Something quite different, a secret.'

'Please yourself,' I said.

'I bought a lovely dress yesterday,' Catherine announced.

'Several,' I said.

'Which one did you like best?'

'I can't remember.'

'Typical male,' said Leee disparagingly.

'I was too busy to notice,' I said.

'Too busy peeping into the girl's changing rooms, I bet.' Leee was enjoying himself.

'Now don't you start teasing,' said Catherine.

When we'd finished dinner I took my new threads back to my suite.

'Will you knock for me at a quarter to nine?' asked Catherine as I left.

'My pleasure.'

'Such a gentleman,' said Leee. 'See you later, Nick. Be good.'

10

I went back to my room and turned on the TV. Another soap. I turned down the volume and went through to the bathroom for a shower. When I got back, the soap was still grinding on. I switched off the TV and lit a cigarette.

I tried on my new suit and, as I knew it would, it fitted perfectly. I managed a reasonable job with the bow tie but I remembered better times when someone would have been around to tie it for me. *C'est la vie.*

I knocked on Catherine's door at eight forty-five precisely. She was sitting alone in the room. She stood as I entered. Her dress was something else. It was made of raw silk and was exactly the colour of her hair. Standing there, she looked like a statue carved out of pure gold. The dress was high-collared with long buttoned sleeves, but the cut of the skirt, which joined like the petals of a flower at the front and showed a lot of inner thigh, took any decorum out of the style.

'You don't think I'll be too warm do you?' she asked.

'You won't,' I said. 'But I might.'

'What a lovely thing to say.' She walked over and kissed my cheek. I've had slaps that were less devastating.

'Where's Leee?' I asked.

'In the bathroom, getting ready. He'll be ages yet. He's much worse than me. Let's go downstairs and see what's happening. I've got the collywobbles. It seems like months since I've been seen in anything but black.'

'Come on then, Miss Pike.' I offered her my arm.

'Too kind, sir,' she said as she took it, and together we walked to the lift.

Courtneidge and Constance were stationed in the hall as greeter and cloakroom attendant respectively. Miranda and Vincent were maid and footman, ready with champagne and glasses. Vincent was straitjacketed into a tuxedo, starched shirt and bow tie of his own, and avoided my eye. I began to wonder if my own evening suit was to save embarrassment at the dinner table or to get me into domestic uniform with the least fuss. I pulled at my collar and knew how Vincent felt. I thought that maybe later I'd go in for the Tom Jones unbuttoned collar and tie hanging loose look. See if any women threw underwear at me. Fat chance.

I caught Miranda in the dining room and took a glass each for me and Catherine. 'You look smart,' she said.

'I think I've got you to thank for that.'

'Do you like the suit?'

'Perfect. Thanks for getting the sizes right.'

'I went to Mr Simon's tailor. He fancies himself, you know, a bit trendy.'

'I bet he does.'

'Don't drink too much, I hate to see you ill.'

'That's not ill, Miranda,' I said. 'That's enjoying life. You should know that by now.'

'Just be careful.'

'I promise,' I said, but I would have crossed my fingers if I'd had a hand free.

I took the champagne through to Catherine. 'Still nervous?'

'Yes, does it show?'

'No.'

The front door bell rang. It was just after nine. 'Good luck,' I said. It was bullshit, but it mattered to her, so what the hell. She smiled and smoothed down the skirt of her dress.

First past the post were a pair of post-punk reptiles and their androgynous girlfriends. They were dressed to slaughter in leather and lace and torn tights and that was just the men.

'Nice idea about the suit,' I whispered to Catherine after we'd all been introduced and I'd just had time to forget their names.

'Don't be so stuffy,' she said. 'You look great and there'll be plenty more men who dress formally along later.'

'I hope so,' I said. 'I feel like I should be serving the drinks.'

'You look like you own the place.' She certainly knew how to get round me.

And she was right. The male half of the very next couple to arrive was wearing a very smart tux with satin lapels. The female half was shoehorned into more satin and greeted Catherine like a long-lost friend. 'Darling,' she screamed. 'You look marvellous.' And she launched into raptures about Catherine's frock.

Just then I saw David, Claire and Simon come through the door from the hall. David had on a suit similar to mine and Claire was wearing a cleavage-revealing creation that she had just too much weight on the hips to get away with. Simon wore a white tux and black trousers with a black shirt and white bow tie. He looked like an extra from *Casablanca*.

The woman who was yapping to Catherine yapped herself out. I caught Catherine's eye and looked towards the door. She picked up my signal and excused herself.

'I see the rest of the family decided to attend,' I said.

'I'd better speak to them.' She put on a smile and moved in their direction. I followed like a shadow.

David shook my hand again and Claire nodded to me like a little plastic dog in the back window of a car. Simon studiously ignored both of us.

'Hello, everyone,' said Catherine.

David looked disgusted. 'This really isn't on, you know, Catherine. Whose brilliant idea was it? Yours?'

'Elizabeth's actually,' said Catherine.

'I just don't understand it. And today of all days.'

'Then why did you come?'

'Because we must put up a united front for the sake of my father and the business. If anything that went on this morning leaks out, our shares will crash.'

I thought it was a bit late for him to worry about that after he'd stormed out of the lawyers' office screaming at the top of his voice, but what do I know? I think Claire understood the situation better than anyone. She grabbed him by the arm and hustled him away hissing, 'Come on, dear, we must circulate.'

'You know I hate parties. I need some air already,' he complained, but allowed himself to be dragged off.

'I think I shall circulate too,' said Simon. 'There must be someone interesting to talk to here.' And with that he turned on his heel and walked away.

Catherine looked after him. 'Miserable little fucker.'

I couldn't have agreed with her more and said so. She pulled a funny face.

By that time the guests were coming in thick and fast. I left Catherine to talk to them, captured a bottle of Brut and took up position by the wet bar in the conservatory where I could keep an eye on Catherine and give the people the once-over as they entered and spoke to her. They ran the spectrum of London society. There were Two-Toners for the second time round. Dowagers, dukes, and duchesses. Models, models' boy friends and models' girl friends. Session men, AIDS victims and those you knew were just waiting to be. Minor pop stars, equerries and barrow boys. Space cadets of every ethnic minority and funny farm rejects of all sorts. Catherine knew everyone and everyone wanted to know her.

Elizabeth showed at around ten. She looked gorgeous in a dress of dark red velvet that seemed to add a tint to her auburn hair. Her lips were carmine and stood out against the paleness of her face. She made a beeline for me.

'Enjoying yourself?' she asked.

'Now that you're here.'

'You're being gallant again, Mr Sharman. I bet you're the scourge of the over-twenty-fives' disco in Peckham Rye.' She was calling me Mr Sharman again. Bad sign.

'Are you taking the mickey?'

'Only a bit. Don't be angry – I'm not used to compliments.'

'That surprises me.'

'Most men are scared to speak to me. I've got a reputation as a bit of a bitch.'

'I'm amazed.'

'Now who's taking the mickey?'

I grinned and she grinned back.

'Are you alone?' I asked.

'No, you're here.'

'Funny,' I said. 'I mean, no escort?'

'No, no escort, or husband, or boy friend, or significant other, or live-in or, for that matter, live-out lover.'

I held up my hands in mock surrender. 'Pardon me for asking. I just thought there might be someone.'

'Why?'

'Because you said you were dining out with a friend on the night your father died, and I assumed – '

'You should never assume, Mr Sharman.'

'I know, it was just something in the way you told me.'

'Am I that transparent? Well, yes, I was, but it was no one important. Not now.'

'Forgive me for asking then.'

'It's you who should forgive me, I get a bit touchy.'

'Touch away.'

'No smut, Mr Sharman, not when you're working.'

'And when I'm not?'

'We'll see.'

I grinned again and snagged a glass from behind the bar and poured her a drink. 'Tell me about some of these people,' I said. 'They're all a bit rich for my blood. Too William Hickey, if you know what I mean.'

'I do. What do you want to know?'

'Who's who.'

'There's a copy in the library.'

'I'll get to the book later. For now, just run a few down for me.'

'All right. Where shall I start?'

'Anywhere. Have another drink and let me into a few secrets.'

She held up her glass and I topped it up with champagne.

'I'm afraid they're not very interesting, unless you like sleaziness.'

'I do,' I replied.

'Okay, do you see him over there?' She pointed to a stout, red-faced party in evening dress who was looking down the cleavage of a young woman so intently that he was in danger of spilling his drink. 'That's Sir Stafford Fontaine. He's on the board at Pike's. He likes young girls and old Scotch, not necessarily in that order.' The stout man dragged his eyes away from all that young flesh and, noticing Elizabeth's interest, raised his glass in salute. Elizabeth toasted him back. 'He tried to get my knickers off when I was thirteen. I'm much too old for him now and he's lost interest.'

'Foolish man,' I said.

'Thank you. And over there are a bunch of Pike editorial staff.' She gestured towards a motley bunch of ageing boys and girls in their best suits and frocks. 'By the way they're dressed, we're paying them too much.'

'And by the way they're knocking back the vol-au-vents and champagne, you're not paying them enough.'

'You could be right.'

'I'm enjoying this,' I said.

'Good.'

'Anyone else?' I asked.

'Him over there.' She nodded her head at a ginger-headed seven-footer who was trying to rescue a cigarette end from his glass of Scotch. 'Twenty-fifth in line for the throne.'

From the state of him, I didn't fancy our chances if the other twenty-four bought the farm in a plane crash. 'Good solid stock,' I said. 'And who's the tough guy who's just come in?'

A tall, good-looking man had appeared at the doorway and was looking around the room. He was about thirty with long hair and a tan. He wore a leather jacket that was so worn that most of the hide had been rubbed off leaving a texture like an old man's face. He wore it over a black T-shirt, tight blue jeans and lace-up black boots. A pair of mirrored shades perched on his nose and a cigarette hung from his lips.

'Curtis!' she said. 'Damn.'

'You know him?'

'He was the one of no importance. What the hell is he doing here, and who invited him?'

'Not you?'

'Obviously.'

'Catherine?'

'I very much doubt it.'

'Cool geezer,' I said.

'He certainly thinks so. I imagine he's been rehearsing his entrance in front of the mirror all afternoon.'

'That doesn't impress you?'

'Not any more. It's all right at first, but the novelty soon wears off.'

'I can imagine.'

'And he thinks he's God's gift.'

'Is he?'

'To a certain kind of woman.'

'Not you.'

'No, I decided I like my diamonds a trifle smoother.'

'But not much.'

'No, not much.' And she smiled at me. It was one of those smiles that hits you low in the stomach and leaves you breathless. It can be addictive. I liked it.

'You're staring again, Mr Sharman.'

'It's a nice view.'

She smiled again. 'Catherine looks great tonight, don't you think?'

'So do you,' I said, refusing to be sidetracked.

'Thank you.'

As if she realised we were talking about her, Catherine looked over from where she was talking to the very tall, minor member of the royal family who towered over her with the posture of a praying mantis. She waved, excused herself and came towards me. Curtis moved in and blocked her way. She looked at him in surprise. Elizabeth made as if to move towards them. 'Leave this to me,' I said. 'It's what you're paying me for. Mingle, it's your party. I'll catch you later.' I squeezed her arm and pushed through the crowd and went up to Curtis and Catherine.

', , , I want to see her. but she refuses to speak to me,' he was saying as I got close.

'Who can blame her?' asked Catherine.

'That's why I came.'

'But you weren't invited,' she said.

'Simon called and told me you were entertaining. I jumped straight in the car and came over. I couldn't miss one of your famous parties.'

'He would,' Catherine said bitterly. 'I wish Simon would mind his own business.'

'Trouble, Miss Pike?' I asked.

Curtis slowly turned and looked me up and down through his

sunglasses. 'Who's the monkey in the funny suit?' he asked. I liked him a lot for that.

'This is Nick Sharman,' said Catherine. 'He's looking after a few details about the estate for us.' That story was getting lamer by the hour.

'I just bet he fucking well is,' said Curtis.

'Did I hear you say that he wasn't invited?' I asked, ignoring Curtis and his mouth.

'Simon asked him,' said Catherine, with a catch in her voice. 'It's all right.'

'Are you sure?' I asked.

'She said so, didn't she?' interrupted Curtis.

For the first time I acknowledged him directly. 'Are you talking to me?' I said. 'Or chewing a brick?'

'You are scraping the barrel, Catherine,' said Curtis. 'What gutter did you drag this vermin from?'

I spoke to Catherine. 'I'll put him out if you like.'

'Just try,' said Curtis.

'No, it's all right, Mr Sharman. Let him stay.'

'If you say so, Miss Pike.'

'And get lost. I want to talk to the lady in private,' said Curtis.

I raised an eyebrow in Catherine's direction.

'Don't worry,' she said.

Curtis grinned and stuck a Rothman into the grin.

'I'll be close,' I said.

'That's reassuring,' said Curtis. 'Give me a light before you go, will you, Sharman?'

I hesitated, then pulled out my lighter and burnt out the end of his cigarette. I noticed that I wasn't shaking at all outside. I smiled and backed away like a good flunky.

As I did so, I felt a tug on my sleeve and looked round. There, standing next to me, wearing an orange dress that was tight enough to display every bump and hollow of her figure was Fiona. 'Hello, Nick Sharman.'

'Hello yourself. What's cooking?'

'My feet in these bleeding shoes,' she replied.

I looked down at her legs which, believe me, was no chore. Her feet were jammed into a pair of orange high heels with platform soles that were so extreme as to be almost surgical. 'That bastard swore they were fives,' she said. 'But I bet they're fours with the size rubbed off.'

'Very stylish,' I said.

'Don't take the piss. They're what I wear.'

'So what are you doing here?' I asked. 'Something told me last night that you weren't number one on the local chart.'

'With a bullet, maybe,' she said. 'No, I'm here with some right honourable friend of Elizabeth Pike's. He's a drag. He can't get it up. He's always snorting shit. Too much stimulation can be bad for the bollocks. I only came to see you. You never phoned me.'

'You only gave me the number the other night,' I protested.

'Most men I give my number to ring me the next day.'

'I'm not most men.'

'And I bet you ain't a collator or whatever bullshit you said you were either. Are you sure you're not Old Bill?'

'I'm sure,' I said.

'You used to be?'

I knew she wasn't going to leave it alone. 'All right, Fiona,' I said, 'I give in. I was a copper once.'

'I knew it, see, I'm never wrong. So why are you really here?'

'Security.'

'For those two?' I assumed she meant Elizabeth and Catherine. 'That's right.'

'What are they scared of, the fashion police?'

'Don't be bitchy, Fiona.'

'All right, I won't. Anyway, what were you doing with that creep?'

'Who?'

'Lover boy in the shades. You looked as if he'd stood right on your favourite corn.'

'I was going to throw him out, but Catherine stopped me.'

'Watch it, Nick, he's a right nasty bastard.'

'So am I. Do you want a drink?'

She nodded. I led her over to the bar and I ordered us both a drink. I leant my elbow on the top and watched as Curtis and Catherine had an animated conversation. He grabbed her arm at one point. She shook him off, and her look told me to stay where I was. My stomach was burning the roast beef I'd eaten to charcoal, but I did nothing.

I scanned the crowd for Elizabeth and couldn't see her, but I did notice another tall individual enter the room and peer around myopically.

'Oh Christ, it's the Right Hon,' said Fiona. 'I'd better go and change his incontinence pants for him.'

'Yeah,' I said. 'See you.'

'Call me.' She put down her glass on the bar top and kissed me on the cheek.

'Count on it,' I said, and she was gone.

Eventually Catherine extricated herself from Curtis and came over to me. I could see the sneer on his face as he watched. I squeezed my glass until it almost shattered.

'Don't ever do that to me again,' I said when she reached me.

'I'm sorry, I'm sorry, I'm sorry.' She was obviously agitated. 'It's difficult. Curtis was such a swine to Elizabeth, but she kept going back for more. You never know where you are with those two. One minute she loves him, next minute she hates him.'

'I get the picture,' I said. 'I think we're in a hate mode at the moment.'

'Good, he gives me the creeps.'

'Where's Leee?' I asked.

'Upstairs, still getting dressed. I'll go and hurry him up.'

'I'll come too.'

'No, it's okay. I'm only going to my room. Anyway, Leee would be furious if anyone saw him before his grand entrance.'

'If you're sure.'

'Of course I am. I'll only be a moment. I want you to keep an eye on Curtis and Elizabeth. I don't like them to be in the same room together.'

'Sure,' I said, but nothing more.

I watched her as she left the room. She had a walk that could corrupt a Boy Scout. I turned back and watched Curtis and Elizabeth gravitate slowly towards each other until eventually they spoke. Or at least Curtis spoke and Elizabeth ignored him, standing with a disinterested look on her face and a champagne glass in her hand, staring past him as if he didn't exist. I saw him get more and more excited until he grabbed Elizabeth's shoulder and spun her round. Her glass flew out of her hand and hit the floor. I took off fast, pushing through the bodies that separated us. I grabbed Curtis from behind and put a neck lock on him. He tried to stamp on my foot but I shoved his legs together and pushed him against the wall. 'Leave it,' I said. 'It's not nice.'

'Let me go.' His voice was muffled by the wallpaper. 'Get your dirty hands off me.'

'If you'll be friendly.'

He struggled, but I had him and he knew it.

'Well?'

'All right,' he spat and I let him go.

As he turned, I sensed rather than heard a scream. As I looked for the source, the glass roof of the conservatory imploded in a shower of glass and blood. It was unbelievable, like a bomb had hit the place. I was frozen to the spot.

There were shouts and screams and the crowd parted like the Red Sea under a sea of red. I recognised the golden dress and caught a cry in my throat. Catherine's head and torso crashed through the glass and a shard as long and wide as a butcher's cleaver was forced into a bloody wound in her stomach. She was caught by one of the wooden beams that supported the glass so that she hung down like a piece of meat. Her hair was stained red and covered her face like a curtain. The first gush of blood that had splattered the floor subsided to a stream, then a trickle that dripped from the edges of the material of her dress and ran down the one arm that dangled into the room.

I walked across the empty space left by the crowd and squelched across the gore, feeling the soles of my shoes sticking to the wooden floor. Then slowly the blonde hair peeled from the scalp and flopped to the ground. Someone screamed, and was cut off abruptly as if they'd been slapped. I looked up and as blood dripped onto the shoulders of my jacket I stared into Leee's eyes.

11

I looked for what seemed like hours but was probably only a few seconds, then I snapped back to reality. 'Somebody call an ambulance and the police,' I shouted and turned and ran out of the room and towards the front of the house. The lift was stalled on the top floor. I hammered on the button but it didn't engage the machinery. I swore and took the stairs two at a time. I was breathing hard when I got to the top floor and I bounced off the walls as I ran along the hall to Catherine's room. I slammed open the door and saw Catherine standing on the balcony looking down. When she heard the door hit the wall she straightened up and turned towards me. One hand was covering her mouth and her eyes were wide. 'What happened?' I shouted. 'What did you do?'

'Nothing,' she said. 'Nick, I've done nothing. He was on the roof. He went to pick us a flower each for our hair, from the roof garden, like I wore last night. He said he'd be right back. I was standing here and I heard a noise up there.' She pointed to the ceiling. 'He fell right past me. He was screaming.' Her face crumpled and she launched herself at me and clung on tightly. I could feel her hands working on my upper arms. I held her for a second, then peeled her off and held her at arm's length.

'How do I get up there?'

'There are stairs along the hall, a brown door.'

I hopped and pulled the Baby Browning from its ankle holster, checked the load, slipped the safety and pumped a round into the chamber. I ran to the brown door and up the narrow flight of stairs to an exit set in a sort of hut built on the roof.

The roof was flat with a thigh-high brick-built wall round the edge. The wall had an additional safety fence of wire mesh supported by metal brackets sunk into the brick. Dead chimneys broke the smoothness of the metalled roof and someone had made a roof garden with a pair of rose-covered archways, ceramic pots, hanging baskets full of beautiful gardenias on the hut and the sides of the chimneys, and boxes full of flowers on trestle tables. There was even a postage stamp of a lawn. The roof was a mixture of light and shadow and I trod lightly as I went over to the back of the house where the mesh was broken and hung down like a veil. There were several spilled plant pots and, in case of footprints, I avoided disturbing the earth and looked carefully over the parapet. I swallowed as I saw Leee's body still half in and half out of the conservatory roof and I wondered why the hell no one had got it down.

I heard sirens from the street and walked back and peered over the ledge at the front of the house just in time to see the tops of an ambulance, a squad car and a panda arrive together with blue lights flashing. They sprawled over the blacktop beneath me like toys and the traffic in Curzon Street started to jam up behind them in both directions. Doors opened and slammed and boots clattered on the pavement as the foreshortened uniformed figures pounded towards the front door. I holstered the gun and went back to the door at the top of the stairs.

Catherine was standing at the bottom of the flight. She was shaking and her right hand was fisted and rubbing into the palm of her left as if she was trying to wear off the skin. I had no time to be pleasant. 'What the fuck is going on, Catherine? Why was Leee in your dress?' I looked at her and corrected myself. 'A dress like yours. What were you up to?'

'It was a joke, a bit of fun. We used to do it when we went out sometimes. Leee loved dressing in women's clothes. He's my size. He used to borrow clothes from me. Tonight we thought we'd make an entrance. Just for a joke.'

And then she cracked, like a nutshell. Tears filled her eyes and she sobbed and began to hit herself with her right hand, still doubled into a fist. She got a couple of good whacks in before I caught her wrist and grabbed her into my arms. I held her so tightly she couldn't move. She struggled, then went as stiff as an ironing board. Finally she let herself go and I had to hold her upright.

I heard footsteps along the corridor and a uniformed police sergeant and constable came round the corner at a brisk gallop. They skidded to a halt and looked at me over Catherine's shoulder. 'Good evening, sir,' said the sergeant. 'Anything I can do to help?'

'You can stand by this door and not let anyone go up who shouldn't. I think someone was pushed off the top a few minutes ago.'

Catherine sobbed again.

'This is Miss Catherine Pike,' I went on. 'Her late father owned this house. My name is Sharman, I'm her bodyguard. I'm going to take her to her room. Your superior officers will need to talk to her and I'd like her to have a few minutes to calm down. The man who fell was a friend of hers.'

'Man?' said the sergeant. 'It looked like a woman.'

'Look closely, Sergeant.' I began to lead Catherine away.

'Just a minute, sir.'

I turned. 'Yes?'

'The constable will accompany you. Just to be on the safe side.'

'Of course,' I said.

'Go with them, Webb, and be polite,' said the sergeant.

'Yes, Sarge,' said the uniformed constable.

We took Catherine to her room and when she was sitting down quietly, I said to the uniform, 'I won't be a minute.'

'Now, sir, you'll have to stay here … '

I turned and walked out. I heard the copper call me back but I kept going to the top of the main stairs. The lift was gone. I looked down and it was sitting on the ground floor.

12

Within ten minutes the police were all over the place like a big blue security blanket.

I was put into a room in the basement next to the kitchen with only a PC for company for forty minutes, while the scene of crime officers checked the body and the roof. Then I was taken into the dining room for a little chat.

There were two coppers in the room. One very young, one much older. I didn't know them. They knew me, or at least about me. I could tell by the way they examined me like an exhibit under glass.

'Sit down, Mr Sharman,' said the older of the two, who was sitting at the head of dining table. He was between fifty and fifty-five, a typical career detective. Hard as nails, and twice as prickly. He had a sharp, lined face with deep-set blue eyes that had seen everything rotten the world had to show, several times over. His hair was grey and thin and needed a cut badly. He wore a zippered, many-pocketed jacket that looked as if it came from *House of Nylon*, and slacks and shoes from Burton's. On the polished table in front of him was an ashtray with a cold pipe lying in it, a packet of Dutch rolling tobacco, a lined shorthand pad and a pencil with a chewed end. He indicated a chair next to him.

'I'm Sutherland,' he said. 'That's Endesleigh.' He didn't mention rank. I took him for an inspector at least. The other copper looked no older than eighteen with a swoop of blond hair that kept falling into his eyes. I imagined he was a D/C on his first biggie. He was dressed in a sharp grey worsted suit with no bagginess at the knees or shininess on the elbows. He was standing at the window looking through a gap in the curtains and turned at the sound of his name. He gave me the once-over and grunted. When he'd seen all he wanted to see, he turned back.

I said nothing.

The silence stretched as Sutherland studied me and Endesleigh studied the outside world.

The older man broke the silence. He was icily polite. As far as he was concerned the formalities were over. Niceties never came into it. 'Tell us what you know about what happened here tonight,' he said.

'About as much as you, I imagine,' I said. 'Next to nothing.'

He looked over at the young policeman again, then back to me.

'Tell me anyway,' he said.

I told him, right from the beginning. I left out the bits about the death threats, although by then I was sure they existed in some shape or form. I'd save them for later. I told him everything else. It didn't take long.

After I'd finished he sat back in his chair and played with the pencil. He thought for a minute or two then leaned forward and spoke. 'When you took this job on, did you believe that either of the Misses Pikes' lives were in danger?'

'No.'

'So why take the job?'

'I needed the money.'

'That was all?'

'Yes.'

'And you thought there was nothing to it?'

I shrugged. 'I just thought that Elizabeth was neurotic, her or Catherine, or both, and rich enough to pander to any neuroses they had.'

'But you came prepared.'

'Sorry?' I said.

The younger policeman turned away from the window and came over and put my .357 Magnum on the table in front of me. He'd been holding it, hidden from me all the time. It was still in its holster but I imagined that someone had unloaded it. I had known that if anyone good went through the room they'd find it. These guys were good, it was their job. The younger man was careful not to scratch the lustre of the table. That was his job too.

Sutherland shook his head as if in disbelief. 'You're in trouble,' he said. 'I think we should lock you up.' The Browning on my ankle felt as big as a tree stump. He was right, I was in trouble.

'Aren't we being a bit hasty?' asked Endesleigh. Sutherland and I both looked at him.

'What do you mean?' asked Sutherland. As if he didn't know and they hadn't worked this little sketch out while I was cooling my heels in the basement.

'Mr Sharman's in trouble, as you rightly say,' said Endesleigh. 'But he could help us and get himself out of trouble.'

'Help us? How? He's nothing, a fucking dog-washer,' said Sutherland.

Endesleigh looked pained. 'Aren't you being a bit hard on him? He used to be in the job. He knows what we want to know and the people here seem to trust him.'

'Trust him!' said Sutherland. 'I wouldn't trust him to tell me the right time.'

'What have we got to lose? We've got the gun and we can bang him up any time.'

Put like that, it made sense, but Sutherland made a show of holding his brow like it was a big decision. I knew it was a foregone conclusion. They'd got me by the nuts and we all knew it.

'Okay,' said Sutherland at length. 'But it's on your head and your responsibility.'

Neatly done, I thought. Divide the opposition and give me a mate to spill my heart out to. A bit of psychology never hurt anyone.

'Right, Mr Sharman,' said Sutherland. 'We're going to give you a break, but remember you'd better be a good boy or we'll have you round the nick before your feet touch the ground, understand?'

I understood all right. I nodded and the atmosphere in the room relaxed a little, but only a little.

Endesleigh played good cop. He sighed like a man being kept from a comfortable bed. 'Unpleasant business, this,' he said.

'Tell that to Leee,' I said.

'Clive,' said Sutherland.

'What?'

'Clive Simpson was his name,' he explained. 'Clive Simpson from Honor Oak. That's the name on his birth certificate. The local boys have been to see his mother.'

'You were quick.'

'Sometimes, Mr Sharman, sometimes. His flatmate was at home and we got his mother's address. Changed his name by deed poll to Leee Monroe. Apparently Marilyn Monroe was his favourite film star.'

'It's a free country,' I said.

'I'm not disputing that. Bit of a funny boy, wouldn't you say? You knowing him and all.'

'I met him twice,' I said.

'But you had his card in your drawer upstairs.'

They had been thorough.

'He gave it to me when we met for the first time the night before last. Lots of people give me their cards.'

'I'm sure they do. But it's a coincidence that he gave you his two days ago, and now he's dead, wouldn't you say? Fancied a new hairstyle, did you? Or was he your dope dealer? We found all sorts in his handbag. Coke, dope, uppers, sleepers.'

'Neither. He knew a lot about this family. I was going to pick his brains.'

'They're all over the conservatory floor,' said Sutherland. 'Pick away.'

'Not funny. He was all right.'

'So who killed him?' asked Endesleigh.

'I don't know,' I said. 'Someone who thought that Leee was Catherine, I suppose.'

'Did you know about all this dressing up business?' asked Endesleigh.

'No.'

'Catherine Pike kept you right in the picture then?' said Sutherland.

'It's hardly something you drop casually into the conversation. It was a joke, a gag.'

Endesleigh looked at me. 'It went wrong, didn't it?'

'Yes,' I said. 'Especially for Leee.'

'It could have been suicide,' said Sutherland.

'You don't commit suicide when you're getting a flower for your hair,' I said, 'and if you've spent all evening getting tarted up like a dog's breakfast, and you're looking to make a big entrance like he was. I don't see you suddenly getting a fatal attack of the guilts about your life style or not being able to pay the gas bill and knocking down all that safety mesh and doing the big jump.'

'I wouldn't know about that,' said Sutherland. 'Must be funny,' he went on, 'strapping your bollocks up like that. They pull them right tight up their arseholes, apparently.'

'And you would know about that.'

'Don't be fucking clever, Sharman,' Sutherland growled. 'Let's go through it all again, now you're on our side, so to speak. And

I warn you, if I find out you're holding anything back I'll process you myself and enjoy every minute of it.'

I think he meant it too. I loosened my tie. 'I don't know much,' I said. 'Just what I've been told, really. I've only been here for a couple of days.'

'Then tell us what you do know,' said Sutherland.

I went through the whole story again. I still didn't tell them about the death threats. I wanted to speak to Elizabeth and Catherine first.

'So the old man's dead, and the will's up in the air, and the future of the whole company is in jeopardy. And we're not talking about a corner shop here,' said Sutherland. 'And then some silly little poof, all dressed up like the girl who's caused all the fuss, is killed, murdered. Very confusing.'

I couldn't have agreed more.

'And who's right in the middle of it,' he went on, 'but you, Sharman. And from what I know, where you go, trouble follows.'

'Just trying to earn a crust, guv.'

He looked around the dining room, and by so doing took in the whole house. 'You'll get more than a crust here,' he said. 'So Mister ex-detective constable, what do you think?'

'It was a suicide?' I said. 'Robert Pike's, I mean. There's no doubt about that, is there?'

Sutherland looked at Endesleigh. Endesleigh looked back and said, 'As far as we know. Open and shut, as the saying goes.'

'I don't know,' I said. 'Give me a chance to find out. Have you spoken to anyone else tonight?'

'We've had words with a few people, including Elizabeth Pike, and we're off to see the other one after we've finished with you.'

'Don't leave it too late.'

'We've got all night.'

'She hasn't, she's had a nasty shock.'

'Not as nasty as Simpson had.'

You couldn't argue with that. 'I suppose with all this,' it was my turn to look round the room, 'and with the people involved, this will be a priority case.'

'You could say that,' said Sutherland.

'So they'll be bringing in the big guns in the morning,' I said.

'Maybe. That's why we need a quick result.'

'Or a mole in the house.'

'Precisely.'

'Don't tell your guv'nors who it is or they might not agree.'

They chewed that one over for a bit, ate it up and spat it out. Then Sutherland came from another angle. 'Who was in the conservatory when Simpson came through the roof?'

'I've already told you.'

'Tell us again.'

'Me, Elizabeth, Vincent, he's the chauffeur. Miranda, she's one of the maids. The geezer I was holding against the wall – Curtis. And a bunch of other people I could point to. I don't know their names. Fontaine was one, and the girl he was with.'

'What was the fight about?' asked Sutherland.

'Curtis was giving Elizabeth Pike a hard time. Technically it was an assault. I just evened things up a bit.'

'He says you jumped him from behind, and technically you assaulted him.'

'Police training,' I said. 'And somehow I don't think he'll be pressing charges.'

'Don't be funny, Sharman,' said Endesleigh. 'You're a long way from being out of the woods yet, remember.'

I remembered the Browning and shut up.

'Were the other members of the family there?' Sutherland again.

'I didn't see them. They were there earlier. Ask Elizabeth, she might remember.'

'We did, she didn't. We'll get around to everyone else in the morning. What we want you to do is nose around. Make yourself busy. We'll keep in close touch. We want this cleared up quickly.

It doesn't look good on the sheet.'

Endesleigh pulled an oblong of pasteboard from his breast pocket. He picked up the pencil from the table and wrote something on the back. He handed the card to me.

'Here's another card for your collection,' he said. 'Don't leave this one lying around.'

I looked at him, then the older man, then the card. I couldn't believe what I was reading, and I looked at Endesleigh again. I could still swear he was no more than a kid. 'Detective Inspector,' I said.

'That's right. This is Sergeant Sutherland.'

'But I thought – '

'Don't think, Sharman,' said Endesleigh. I remembered that Elizabeth had said something similar when I'd last spoken to her. It seemed to be the way the whole case was going.

'That's good,' I said. 'I like that. Clever. Puts people off their stroke.'

'It does, doesn't it?' said Endesleigh. 'You can go now.'

'What about my gun?'

'We'll look after that for you. A hostage to fortune, as it were. Don't worry, we'll keep it oiled.'

'Cheers,' I said.

'Goodnight, Sharman,' said the detective inspector. 'Sleep tight.'

I thought about Leee coming through the glass roof of the conservatory with a bang that almost made my heart stop, and the blood that was bright orange under the lights, and the bits of him all over the floor and I doubted that I would.

''Night,' I said, and got up and left.

Miranda was sitting on a chair outside the dining room and the young copper who had been looking after me was trying to look up her skirt. She had been crying and had a handful of wet tissue. 'Hello, Miranda,' I said.

'Hello, Mr Sharman. I've got to talk to the policeman. I'm scared.'

'Don't be, they're all right and there'll be a policewoman in with you.'

'Yes, I know, I've been talking to her. She's nice. She's gone off to make some tea.'

'Great, you've got nothing to worry about then.'

'It was horrible, Mr Sharman. I can't stop thinking about it.'

'I know.'

'I thought it was Miss Catherine.'

'I know,' I said again. 'I'll tell her you asked after her if you don't see her first.'

'That's all right,' Miranda said. 'She'll be busy.'

'Not that busy.'

'I mean she'll be upset. That Leee was funny, they loved each other, you know.'

'I know.' She started crying again.

'Have you got a handkerchief, Constable?' I asked.

'No.'

'Find some tissues, will you?'

'I'm not bloody "Boots".'

I looked him up and down but before I could give him any verbal a young policewoman came round the corner from the direction of the stairs to the kitchen with a tray of tea things. 'Got any tissues?' I asked.

'Yes, in my bag. I'll look after Miranda.'

'I'm going upstairs. Will you get Miranda to bed soon, Miss? Try and keep them in there on a lead,' I said to the policewoman.

She smiled. 'I will,' she said. See, not all coppers are bastards.

I went upstairs using the lift. The sergeant I'd met earlier was outside Catherine's door. 'You can't go in,' he said. 'The doctor is in there. But don't worry, there'll be someone here all night.'

'That's good. Are her windows locked?'

'Yes, sir.'

'Goodnight then, Sergeant. See you in the morning.'

'Not me, sir. I'm off duty in an hour but someone will take over.'

'Fine,' I said and went into my room.

13

_____

I undressed and took off the Browning. I put it in the drawer of the bedside table with my watch. It was ten to one when I climbed into bed and, despite what I thought, I did sleep straight away. I was bone tired after two days of drinking and being hungover.

I came to when someone slapped me in the face and kept slapping. There was a bright light in my eyes and at first I thought the police had come back and decided to change their tactics and bring the rubber hoses. I struggled to sit up and got pushed back onto the mattress hard. Someone had turned the bedside lamp shade round and the bulb was shining straight into my face. I remember saying something bright like 'What?' or 'Who?' but another slap shut me up and I lay still and tried to focus on what was going on.

I was on the bed covered with a single sheet and dressed just in shorts. The room was dark and I had no way of knowing what time it was, whether it was still dark outside or whether the curtains had been closed against daylight. There were at least two other people in the room with me. In the bleed of light from the bulb I could make out their shadowy figures. One was sitting in a chair drawn up close to the lefthand side of the bed, the second was standing on the other side of the bed close enough for me to hear him breathe. I guessed it was him who had been slapping. The light reflected onto an automatic pistol with a long, vented silencer screwed onto the muzzle that the seated man held in his hand. The gun was cocked. The hand holding it was wearing a black, shiny glove which met a striped shirt cuff emerging from a dark sleeve, almost completely covering the gold bracelet of a wrist watch.

I lay still and felt my heart hammering in my rib cage.

'Don't make a sound,' said a voice from the other side of the room. It didn't come from either of the men beside the bed. Three then. The voice had a Cockney accent. No, not real Cockney. Australian, that was it. I wasn't surprised. I squinted into the light but all the faces were invisible in the shadows. 'Bit early for trick or treat,' I said. My mouth was dry and I licked at my lips.

'Funny man,' said the standing figure beside the bed. He had an Australian accent too.

'We've come to give you a message to pass on to Catherine Pike,' said the man with the gun.

'And a message for yourself,' said the man standing by my bed.

I said nothing.

The sitting man spoke again. 'Tell her that she owes us what we agreed. We had a deal and she's reneging. We don't like that.'

I could feel sweat running off my body and dampening the sheets.

'And as for you,' the standing man said, 'you're in the way. This thing is nothing to do with you. Give her the message and go home. You're playing in the wrong ball park.'

I licked my lips again. 'I don't know what you're talking about,' I said.

'We don't expect you to. Just pass on the message and get lost.'

The man in the chair brought the gun up and pointed it into my face. I instinctively pushed the back of my head deeper into the pillow. 'I was all for killing you now,' he said. 'But calmer heads prevailed. I won't listen next time.'

'Leave him,' said the voice of the man I couldn't see.

'There's a policeman outside,' I said.

'We're terrified,' the geezer with the gun said. 'One unarmed guy, half asleep. Give him a shout. You'll be dead before he can move and he'll be dead the moment he sticks his head round the door. Just do as you're told.'

'Why don't you tell Catherine yourself?'

'Give her this.' He tossed a brass-jacketed bullet onto the bedside table. It glittered as it rolled across the polished wood and hit the base of the lamp with a click. 'Tell her there's another like it with her name on it. There's one for you too if you're not out of here by tomorrow night.'

'Which one of you is Lorimar?' I asked. It was a guess, but it seemed to hit the spot.

'What did you say?' The invisible man again, but now I could see him, or at least the shape of him, over by the window. For the first time he didn't seem so sure of himself.

'You heard,' I said. I addressed the figure. 'Is it you?'

There was no answer.

'I thought so,' I said. 'You killed Leee.'

'Yes,' he said coldly.

'What's this all about?' I asked.

'A business deal, pure and simple. We kept our part of the bargain and she didn't. We aren't happy about that. That's all you need to know. In fact, the less you do know, the better. We're going now. I advise you to stay put. We've got that little belly gun of yours. If you want to raise a commotion, be our guest, but someone will get hurt and it might be you. Now get up and go to the bathroom.'

I did as I was told. The standing man slid into the shadow and I swung myself out of bed and went to the bathroom door. 'Get inside and stay there,' one of them ordered. Once again I did as I was told. I tried the bathroom light but the bulb must have been removed. I stood in the pitch dark for what seemed like hours but could only have been a couple of minutes. I opened the door and the bedroom was empty. I went back into the room. The bedside lamp had been turned off and the curtains were open, allowing the pre-dawn light to dribble through the window. I went over and peered through it without moving the curtain. The fire escape was as empty as if they'd never been there.

I closed the curtains and switched on the main light. The room looked exactly as when I went to bed. My watch was still in the bedside table drawer. It was 3 a.m. The Browning and its ankle holster were gone. I wasn't having a lot of luck with firearms that night.

Though the room was warm and muggy, the sweat drying on my body was cool and I went back to the bathroom for a towel. Light from the bedroom leaked through the open door and I fumbled around until I eventually found one and rubbed myself down. I fetched cigarettes from the sitting room and lit one and sat on the bed. Things were starting to happen. Things were getting serious. I had been lied to and I wanted to know exactly what was going on. The police presence precluded my jumping straight in with my size tens. I'd have to be patient. I was no longer tired so I sat up for the rest of the night smoking and thinking.

14

I sat on the bed and watched all-night TV and drank the refrigerator dry of soft drinks. I dozed, then came awake. Leee's death and the film I was watching and my dreams and what Lorimar and his murderous little crew had said ran into each other like the layers of a cake until long after dawn when I got dressed and went downstairs.

There was a different copper guarding Catherine's door. He had found a delicate Chippendale chair and was slumped over it like a lumpy schoolboy, but straightened as I came into the corridor. 'All right?' I asked.

'All right,' he replied in an unfriendly way. My reputation had gone before me or else the chair was as uncomfortable as it looked.

'No chance of anyone getting in last night with you lot about,' I said. He mumbled something unintelligible in reply. 'Keep up the good work,' I said and walked on past. Christ, I could have been murdered in my bed for all he knew. I didn't ask him about Catherine. He would be the last to know. Cannon fodder.

I went down to the dining room. It was barely six and the room was empty. No coppers, no coffee, and the dining chairs were back in their original positions. I needed to see Elizabeth but I needed coffee more. I went down to the kitchen. Courtneidge was standing next to a cold oven drinking from a huge white china mug. 'Good morning,' I said.

'Not for us.'

'Of course not.' I could see he needed to have someone listen to his gripes.

'Cook has taken to her bed and is threatening to walk out later. Miranda and Constance aren't even down yet.'

'The police kept them up late.'

'They should be here,' he said as if I hadn't spoken.

I shrugged, he wasn't interested in what I had to say. He was too wrapped up in himself. 'Got any coffee?'

'Instant, or there's tea in the pot. I must apologise but I have to prepare breakfast for the family on my own. There'll be fresh coffee later.'

'Does it matter?'

'Of course it matters. Standards always matter.'

'Come off it, Courtneidge,' I said. 'There's a kid spread all over the conservatory floor. Does it matter if the family have to make do with cornflakes instead of that spread that's usually chucked away?'

'It matters to me.'

I shook my head and spooned some coffee into a mug, added milk and sugar and hot water. It tasted just fine.

'You must excuse me now, Mr Sharman. I have lots to do.'

'Want a hand?'

'Thank you, no.'

I knew when I wasn't wanted and took my cup upstairs. The door to the conservatory was taped off and another uniform was leaning against the wall outside. I went into the drawing room and out onto the paved patio. It was already hot and the early mist had all but evaporated. A tarp had been stretched over the conservatory roof and the blinds drawn. I lit a cigarette and perched on the low wall that separated the levels of the patio and drank my coffee.

I ground out the cigarette and had a sudden feeling I was being watched. I shivered involuntarily under my shirt and turned slowly to look up the back wall of the house. The sunlight bounced off the windows and made me squint but on the second floor I thought I saw a face at one of the windows. I looked again and the face was gone.

I took my cup back into the drawing room and left it on the table there and went looking for life. I knocked on Elizabeth's sitting-room door. She answered and I opened it. She was sitting in the bright sunlight in front of an open bureau writing in a leather-covered book. Newspapers were scattered over the sofa. She closed the book when she saw me and turned in her seat to face me. 'Good morning,' I said.

'Is it?'

'How's Catherine?'

'Not so good. I called out her doctor last night. She was close to a breakdown. He gave her something to make her sleep. If she's no better this morning, I'm to call him again. Christ, what a mess.'

'I had visitors last night,' I said.

'What kind of visitors?'

'Friends of Catherine's.'

'What do you mean? What kind of friends?'

'Bad friends with guns. Bad friends who killed Leee.' I took the bullet that the Australian with the gun had thrown onto the table out of my pocket. 'Bad friends who left this as a warning. And one of the bad friends was named Lorimar, and he knows Catherine, In fact, according to him, she owes him money on some kind of deal.'

Elizabeth's face paled.

'Did you know that she knew Lorimar?' I asked.

'No.'

'Are you sure?'

'Of course I'm sure.'

'I'd hate to think you've been having me on, Elizabeth. Someone's been lying and I want to know who. My visitors gave me a message for Catherine. I need to talk to her, to both of you.'

'Not now, Catherine is resting. She's not up to it yet. There are reporters crawling all over the place. The papers are full of it. Murder, cross-dressing. They're having a field day.'

'Who can blame them?' I said. 'Imagine what they'd make of my visitors.'

Her face went even paler if that were possible. 'You won't,' she said.

I shook my head. 'No. You can trust me.'

'I knew I could,' she said. 'We'll talk later, I promise.'

'Okay, I'll wait, but I don't like waiting. What's on your agenda this morning?'

'The police are coming back at eight. The conservatory is going to be cleaned and repaired as soon as possible and we'll get back to normal.'

'Do you think you ever will?' I said. 'I don't want to talk to the law. They gave me a hard enough time last night. I'm going out. I've got to do some thinking. I'll be back later to speak to Catherine, ready or not.' I got up and left the room without waiting for a reply.

I let gravity carry me downstairs and met Miranda on the first-floor landing. 'How are you feeling?' I asked.

'Awful,' she replied. 'I want to get away from here.'

'I know how you feel.'

Her face puckered as she remembered. 'There was so much blood,' she said.

'Try not to think about it.' I touched her arm. 'You shouldn't be working today. Can't you get some time off?'

'I could, but the place is a shambles and I don't want to leave the family.'

I didn't know what to say to that, so I said nothing. 'I need some air,' I told her. 'I'm going for a walk.'

'You can't go out the front. There are reporters and photographers and TV cameras all over the place.'

'I'll use the back way.'

'Mr Courtneidge has already chased some reporters away from there too. They were going through the dustbins.'

'That's about their speed,' I said. 'They won't bother me.' But I didn't want to meet them. I didn't want to meet anyone. 'What time do you make it?' I asked.

She looked at her wristwatch. 'Seven o'clock.'

'Do me a favour. Go downstairs and at exactly five past open the front door. Don't go out or show yourself. Just keep the door open for a minute or two, okay?'

'Why?'

'Anyone at the back will come running and I can slip away.'

'All right, Mr Sharman.'

'You're an angel, Miranda. I'll owe you one.'

We went down to the hall and Miranda waited while I went down to the kitchen where the smell of bacon frying filled the air. I went out and squeezed past the dustbins. I looked through the railings and there were three guys hanging around smoking and chatting. Two of them had cameras round their necks. I looked at my watch and right on time there was a shout from the end of the mews where it entered Curzon Street. The three newsmen legged it across the cobbles. I smiled and ducked out and away in the opposite direction.

15

I went back to the park. On the way I bought a copy of every morning paper, a cheese sandwich and a black coffee in a styrofoam cup from an entrepreneurial newsagent cum snack bar behind the Hilton. I wandered across to the Serpentine and sat on a bench. I looked at the headlines and drank the coffee and investigated the inside of the sandwich, which was none too clever.

All the late editions of the papers had the story; the tabloids, with the exception of the Pike publications, had it splashed across their front pages. They made a meal of it, too. I found the news as hard to digest as the food I'd bought so I ended up trashing the linens and feeding the processed bread and cheese to the ducks. The coffee wasn't bad, though. I smoked halfway through a pack of Silk Cut as the sun burned across the sky and thought about what had happened the previous night.

I was as jumpy as fuck and well pissed off with everyone with the surname Pike by the time I heard a clock strike eleven somewhere off towards Queensway. I got up and went looking for a boozer. I ended up at a big old gin palace at Scotch Corner. It was empty and anonymous and the staff didn't give a toss about the customers. That suited me down to the ground, except that the beer was warm and about as expensive as they could get away with without being tarred and feathered and run out of Knightsbridge on a rail.

I watered the Becks down with ice until it was drinkable and sat in a quiet corner. As I finished the pack of cigarettes I watched the drinkers rotate in shifts from tourists to grannies on shopping trips to Harrod's, to the wage slaves on their strict lunchtimes. When it got too crowded to move I split back into the one o'clock heat.

I walked across the edge of the park to Curzon Street where there was still a crowd of monkeys with cameras and portable phones and minicams and even the occasional anachronism of a real notebook and well-chewed pencil camped outside the house. I doubled back down to the mews avoiding a couple of hacks, and jumped over the railings before I could be immortalised on film or video.

I went into the coolness of the basement and through to the kitchen where Miranda was standing in front of the oven stirring something savoury in a Teflon saucepan.

'Oh, you're back are you? The police have been looking everywhere for you.'

'They seek him here, they seek him there,' I said.

'You're cheerful.'

'Six bottles of Becks. It'll do it every time.'

'Are you drunk?'

'Miranda, you should get that put on tape.'

'Funny.'

'Not one of my best. Are the Old Bill still around?'

'I think the detectives have gone but there's still an ordinary policeman in the conservatory.'

'Good,' I said. I didn't want to see Endesleigh or his sidekick for a bit. 'What about Catherine and Elizabeth?'

'They're up in Miss Elizabeth's sitting room. I'm making them some soup for lunch.'

'I'll take it up.'

'No, you mustn't.'

'It's okay, trust me.'

'All right,' she said eventually. 'But if you get me into trouble …'

There was an answer to that one but I let it go. 'It'll be okay, I promise. I can handle those two.' At least I hoped I could.

'It's Mr Courtneidge I'm worried about,' she said.

'Where is he?'

'Having a nap. He was up very early and did everything himself this morning. He's dead on his feet.'

An unfortunate choice of expression I thought, but I didn't mention it. 'No problem then,' was what I did say.

She smiled and pulled a conspirational face. 'Go on then.'

'Thanks, and thanks for the diversion this morning. It worked like a charm.'

'Good. I hate those newspaper people. They only want to cause trouble.'

I agreed and watched as she put the soup into a small tureen which she placed on an already prepared tray set with a creamy white cloth, two soup plates, cutlery, a wicker basket of fresh rolls and a china tub of butter. I picked up the whole shebang which, I might add, weighed a ton and made me think that Miranda and Constance must have been stronger than they looked, and took the servants' lift to the second floor. I walked down the corridor. Balancing the tray on one arm, I knocked on Elizabeth's sitting-room door and entered. Elizabeth and Catherine were both on the sofa, deep in conversation. 'Leave the tray on the table,' said Elizabeth without looking up. 'We'll ring when we're finished.'

'Don't let it get cold,' I said.

They both looked up as if they'd been goosed.

'Where the hell have you been and what do you think you're doing with that?' said Elizabeth with an edge of anger in her voice.

'Just saving the staff a job and I told you I was going out. I was

146

finding the atmosphere a little oppressive in here.'

'The police are looking for you,' said Elizabeth.

'So I understand.'

'I suppose they should have combed the local pubs,' said Catherine nastily. She was changing her tune. Obviously Elizabeth had told her about my midnight callers.

'I'm cut to the quick,' I said back. 'But as a matter of fact I did drop in for a livener.'

'More than one, by the sound of it.' Catherine again.

'As if it's any of your business.'

'We're paying you,' said Elizabeth.

'That's another matter. Before we go into all that, I think you've got something to tell me.'

The two women seated on the sofa looked at each other.

'Well, come on,' I said impatiently. 'Spit it out.'

'What do you want to know?' said Elizabeth.

'Why the chicken crossed the road!' I said. 'What the hell do you think I want to know? I want to know what I'm doing here.'

'Trying to bully us,' Elizabeth retorted.

'And obviously not succeeding,' I said. 'Okay, let's take it one step at a time. You told me when you hired me that maybe, just maybe, your father's death wasn't the suicide it was supposed to be. You told me that Catherine was scared, of what you didn't know. You also let me believe she was a sweet, hard-done-by soul, pure as the driven. Now I discover that she was involved all along with someone who was being paid a great deal of money by your late father. So, Catherine, dear, sweet, hard-done-by soul, tell me about it.'

'It's not what you think,' said Catherine.

'Who said I think anything?' I asked. 'And who is this cat Lorimar?'

'One of those men I told you about, my mother's men,' replied Catherine.

'And what is he?'

'Anything he wants to be. A thief, a murderer, a con man. He was working the resort hotels when my mother met him.'

'Doing what exactly?'

'Like I said, anything. Scamming, stealing from rooms. Bunco, anything.'

'And why did Sir Robert start paying him?'

'My mother told Lorimar the whole story one night when she was drunk. He was a good listener. He had to be, doing what he did. He got in touch with my father and threatened to make the matter public.'

'Did your mother know?'

'Of course. I think she actively encouraged him. I told you she hated my father. And we were always broke, even with the money my father sent to us. A little extra didn't hurt.'

'Naughty old mum.'

'But when Elizabeth's mother died, it all stopped,' she went on.

'Not quite. Lorimar said something about a deal last night. A deal with you. What kind of deal was that?'

'I can't tell you.'

'Yes you can.'

'No.'

'Was it something to do with why you disappeared after your mother died?'

She wouldn't look at me.

'It was, wasn't it?' I pressed.

'It was something that happened after I took off,' she said and tears filled her eyes.

I was getting bored with tears. 'Tell me, Catherine,' I said.

'I can't.'

'Of course you can.'

There was a long silence in the room. I watched a fly banging its head against the window. I sympathised. I knew how it felt.

'All right,' said Catherine at last. 'My mother was a drunk and an easy lay. She was running with all sorts of bad company before she died, Lorimar included. He was the last and the worst. I was just a kid and didn't understand, or maybe I did. I told you I had to grow up fast. In some things I was very mature, in others not at all. All I knew was that I hated the people, the men who hung around my mother. They were always trying to get her to go out or pass out from the booze and try it on with me. I told you I was twelve when I lost my virginity. I was raped. Mother wouldn't listen. She wouldn't hear a word against her friends. She didn't believe me, or chose not to. It was horrible.

'The day after she was buried I packed a single bag with clothes and put all the personal papers I could find into another bag and split. I was sixteen years old and didn't have a friend in the world who wasn't a hotel doorman or barman or chambermaid. Can you believe that? That's why I took the papers and the scrapbook, without them I would literally not have existed. I walked out of a hotel in Melbourne and took a bus to Sydney. I had a little money. I was so scared of Lorimar catching up with me, I never even tried to touch the money in my mother's bank. I even paid for the funeral out of my savings.

'I got to Sydney one Saturday morning and hung around the city centre all weekend. Eventually I met some people who were squatting a house and moved in. There were hippies and punks and all sorts there, and there were always drugs around. I got involved. Eventually I got hooked and I started turning tricks for cash. The funny thing is that Lorimar wasn't even looking for me, not then. Then Elizabeth's mother died and the money from my father dried up. Lorimar was furious. He thought he'd got a pension for life. That was when Lorimar started looking. It didn't take him long to find me. I was a permanent fixture at King's Cross by then. He told me that unless I went to England and got in touch with my father and screwed money out of him, he, Lorimar that is, would hurt me, hurt me bad. He would have, too, he's a terrible man. He got me off the game and dried out, and you know the rest.'

'What about drama school?' I asked.

'I went for two terms, then dropped out.'

'And your mother's money.'

'What do you think? Lorimar found out that I could get to it and made me pay every penny over to him.'

'Jesus, Catherine,' I said. 'You mean you came over here just to con your old man?'

'I had no choice. I didn't want to do it. I didn't want anything to do with him, and I hated doing it, believe me. At first I just felt tacky taking the money. And then I got fond of Sir Robert. In the end I loved him. And the more I loved him, the more I hated myself.'

'Why didn't you tell Sir Robert about it if you hated doing it so much? He would have taken care of it.'

'I couldn't, don't you see? My father had already had Lorimar on his back for fifteen years. Do you think I wanted him to know that I'd brought him back to his door again. Anyway, Lorimar would only have twisted it so that it looked like it was my idea. Like mother, like daughter.'

'Did you know about any of this, Elizabeth?' I asked.

'Not until today. I'd never even heard of Lorimar until my father died.'

I believed her. 'And when your father died?' I said to Catherine.

'Lorimar told me he wanted one last payment, then he'd leave me alone. Or else.'

'Or else what?'

'You saw what happened to Leee.'

'Did you know about the will?'

'Of course not.'

'Have you got any money of your own?'

'No.'

'What about your allowance?'

'Lorimar took it. He left me some and took the rest.'

'And the house your father bought for you?'

'Mortgaged.'

'How much does Lorimar want?'

'One million pounds sterling.'

'Nice round figure,' I said. 'Why didn't you tell me all this before, instead of going through that ridiculous charade that probably got Leee killed?'

'I don't know, I was frightened.'

'Not too frightened to go to parties and shopping.'

The tears welled up in Catherine's eyes again. I was beginning to think she could turn them on and off at will.

'Well, I've passed on the message,' I said. 'It's time for me to make my excuses and leave, or else I'm brown bread, that's what I was told.'

'Scared?' sneered Catherine.

'Of course,' I said. 'I saw what they did to Leee too. And did Elizabeth tell you about the little present they left for you?'

'Melodramatic crap.'

'Maybe, maybe not.'

'And are you going to leave?' asked Elizabeth.

'You tell me.'

There was a pause.

'Christ I need a cigarette! Elizabeth,' Catherine smiled sweetly, 'there's a fresh packet in my room, would you mind?'

'I've got some here,' I said.

'I want my own,' said Catherine sharply. Elizabeth looked bemused but got up and left the room anyway.

'Can't we come to some arrangement?' asked Catherine when the door had clicked shut.

'What kind of arrangement?'

'Get real, Sharman,' said Catherine. 'Why do you think we hired you? You kill cunts, don't you? Kill this little lot and you'll get rich in a serious way.'

West End girls; my old mum was right.

'I don't need money that bad,' I said. Oh boy, was my nose going to grow.

'Rubbish,' said Catherine. 'You're broke, Elizabeth checked you out. Do this little job for us and we'll pay you well.'

'If you think I'm a bumpman, sweetheart, you're knocking on the door of the wrong hacienda,' I said. 'Tell the police, they're all over the shop. It's their job to take care of people like them.'

'We don't want to involve the police any more than they already are,' said Catherine.

'That would be difficult I agree,' I said drily.

'Look, Sharman, just name your price.'

'That's your answer to everything, isn't it? You rich fuckers are all the same. I've met your sort before. You think that money takes care of everything.'

'It helps.'

'So they tell me. But too much takes some of the fun out of life, doesn't it? That's why Elizabeth was doing a little hoisting, isn't it? Just for kicks. Hanging out with brass can lead to bad habits.'

'Don't call me brass,' said Catherine.

'Why not, sweet? Does it offend you?' I asked. 'So what should I call you? You tell me, I'll go along.'

'You bastard.'

'You want me to call you that? In public?'

That about did it. She came off the sofa like she had springs in her tail and in her right hand was a nasty-looking blade. She came right at me. The knife tore my shirt and I felt the point skid off my ribs and cut through skin and muscle. There was no pain, just a shock that ran down my side. I caught her arm and twisted it hard. She screamed and the knife hit the carpet. I spun her round and punched her hard on the side of the jaw, hard enough so that her teeth clicked together so loudly that the sound echoed in the room. She hit the carpet with a thud.

16

Just as Catherine hit the carpet the door flew open and Elizabeth appeared, her hand to her mouth stifling a scream.

'For Christ's sake, don't just stand there,' I said. 'I'm bleeding to death here.' And I was. Well, not exactly, but my shirt was soaked with blood and the wound was beginning to hurt, severely. 'Does she always carry a blade?' I asked, and didn't wait for an answer. 'She's fucking lethal, you know that?' I looked at Catherine lying unconscious on the floor. Then I pulled my shirt out of my pants, undid the buttons and looked at my ribs. There was a skinny wound, maybe eight inches long, oozing blood. My side was wet with blood and the waistband of my blue jeans was stained black with it.

Elizabeth was now standing, white-faced, in the middle of the room, shaking.

'Pull yourself together, for God's sake,' I said. 'Have you got anything to bandage this?'

'I'll ring downstairs.'

'Don't be stupid. Do you want everyone to know about it? Haven't you got anything up here?'

'I'll find something,' she said, and went towards the bedroom door.

'Something absorbent,' I said. 'And some Band Aid and disinfectant and something to clean it with.'

She left the room. I picked up the knife and winced at the movement. It was a switchblade with a bone handle and a six- or seven-inch blade that was as sharp as a razor. I unlocked the blade, closed the knife and slipped it into the back pocket of my jeans.

Catherine was breathing heavily. There was a big blue bruise coming up on her chin and the side of her face was swollen. I bent down and checked that her tongue wasn't blocking her windpipe. Her pulse was a little slow but she'd survive.

Elizabeth came back into the room carrying a bowl and a bunch of stuff and a small bottle. I told her to put it down and help me get Catherine onto the sofa. 'Get her feet,' I said. Elizabeth did as she was told and we lifted Catherine onto the cushions. The exertion made me wince and the cut in my side started to bleed worse. 'Now sort this out for me,' I said, looking down at the fresh blood oozing from my wound.

'Is it very deep?' Elizabeth asked.

'No, I don't think so. What've you got?'

'TCP, warm water, lint and tape.'

'You're well prepared. Mind you, you need to be with her about. Is she always armed?' I asked again.

'I've never seen the knife before.'

'It must be a legacy from when she was a working girl,' I said. 'And beware any John who tried to slip away without paying.'

Elizabeth didn't answer. 'Come and sit by the window, in the light,' she said.

It was my turn to do as I was told and she cleaned the wound with the water. 'It's not too bad,' she said. 'But this might hurt a bit.' She splashed disinfectant into the cut and I thought I was going to pass out.

'Christ,' I said. 'It's deeper than I thought.' I wiped tears from my eyes and she covered the wound with clean lint and bound it tightly with tape.

'Are you all right?' she asked.

'I'll live.'

'You should go to hospital. That needs stitches.'

'No thanks. I'm allergic.'

'Please yourself. Will Catherine be all right? She's been out for a long time.'

'She'll be fine. She's just asleep.'

'This is awful,' Elizabeth said. 'I didn't realise what was going on.'

'She did.' I looked over at Catherine's still form. 'She's been winding us both up since this started.'

'She's scared and all alone.'

'Why don't you just pay then?'

'She hasn't got that much cash, and nor have I. Even if Daddy's will wasn't being contested, all the assets are tied up in trust and property and machinery. We couldn't liquidate without a lot of questions being asked, you know.'

I didn't, but what the hell.

'And as things are, it's just impossible,' she went on.

'Even if they got it, I guess they'd be back for more,' I said.

'Do you think so?'

'Count on it – and I think they've got someone in the house.'

'How do you know that?'

'I don't, but they knew that the party was on, and about Leee dressing up as Catherine and the roof garden and me. Work it out for yourself.'

'Who?'

I shrugged and winced again. 'Who knows?'

The side of my body was starting to throb like the motor in an old fridge on full frost and was sending stabs of pain right up behind my eyes. 'Got any pain killers?' I asked. 'Something strong.'

'I've got some prescription stuff.'

'Let's have them, and some booze.'

'There are drinks in the cabinet.'

I went over to the fancy-fronted chiffonnier by the window and opened one of the doors. I found a new bottle of Jack Daniel's, broke the seal and took a hit. The liquor burnt a hole right down to my belt buckle and I took another. Meanwhile Elizabeth went back to her bedroom and reappeared carrying a pill bottle. I flicked off the lid and emptied a pile of DF 118s onto the top of the cabinet. I took two and washed them down with another mouthful of bourbon.

'Be careful, they're strong.'

'I need something strong,' I said. 'It's not every day I get stuck like a pig. If it makes you feel any better, I promise not to operate any heavy machinery this afternoon.'

She gave me a disgusted look and I put the remaining pills back into the bottle and the bottle into my pocket.

'Right,' I said. 'While she's still out of it, let's talk seriously.'

'You've made it perfectly clear you're not interested in helping us.'

'I'm not interested in helping you kill anyone, that's for sure. Do you blame me? But I did take on the job of protecting the pair of you and I do hate being told what to do by anyone.'

'What do you intend doing then?'

'I'm not sure.'

'Kill the lot of them,' said Catherine from the sofa.

I looked over to where she was lying. 'Back in the land of the living?'

'Just about. You pack a mean right.'

'You pack a mean flickknife,' I said. 'How long have you been listening?'

'Long enough.'

Elizabeth went over and sat next to her. 'Are you all right, Catherine?'

'I'll survive. What's our hero going to do? That's more important.'

I looked at the pair of them and made a decision. 'I was given until tonight to split,' I said. 'And they'll be watching. If I stay and anything goes wrong, you know that you could both end up in Holloway? And me down the road in Brixton on remand.'

'You'd have the best lawyers that money can buy,' said Elizabeth.

'That's reassuring,' I said. 'I should just go right now. I've passed on the message, now I should split, go to the law and drop the whole bloody mess into their collective laps and earn some Brownie points for a change. I'm already looking at a twoer for illegal possession of an unlicensed firearm.'

'What?' said Elizabeth.

'You heard. The Bill spun my little garret last night and pulled out a plum.'

'More fool you for not hiding it better,' said Catherine.

'Your concern is touching.'

'Be quiet, Catherine,' said Elizabeth. 'You're not helping.' Then to me, 'What do you propose?'

'I don't know,' I said. 'But I think I'll stick around.'

17

I went back to my room to change my clothes. Someone had made the bed and the blood-spattered DJ was gone. I took off my messed-up shirt and jeans, emptied the pockets and looked around for somewhere to stash them. It was pretty comfortable having servants but I wondered how the boss classes managed to keep anything secret. Perhaps they just didn't care. I ended up rolling the lot into a ball and shoving the bundle into the bottom of my suitcase to rot. I put the knife and the pills in my bureau drawer and checked the bandage. There was a little seepage of blood and the wound was hurting like hell. It pissed me off to think that the silly bitch could have topped me. In fact I was beginning to think that the pair of them were half crazy and it occurred to me that they wouldn't worry too much if I was stretched out on a cold slab somewhere.

I gingerly flannelled the sweat and blood off my body, wrapped a towel around my hips and sat on the bed. I found Endesleigh's card and gave him a bell. I tried his office number and got straight through to his desk. 'Endesleigh,' he said.

'Afternoon, Mr Endesleigh,' I said. 'Nick Sharman.'

'Sharman, I was looking for you this morning.'

'I needed some time to think.'

'How about a night in the cells? Would that do?'

'Not that much time and I don't think I'd find the surroundings conducive. I need to see you.'

'Got something for me?'

'Definitely.'

'I'll come round later.'

'No, not here. There's a boozer in the market, The Shepherd's, know it?'

'Yeah.'

'Seven?'

'I'll be there.'

'Cheers,' I said, and hung up.

The pills and the booze were starting to work. My side felt numb and so did the area between my ears. I lay back on the bed and closed my eyes.

I woke after six. My head was banging like a cheap in-car stereo and my side felt as if it had been bound with a red-hot electric cable. I looked at the bandage and it was stained an attractive mixture of rust red and puss yellow.

I cleaned my teeth, shaved, took two more pain killers and put on a clean shirt, a tie with a pattern like an explosion in a fruit salad cannery and my grey suit. I wasn't going to be jumping over any railings for the next few days and if there were any photographers still out front I wanted to look my best. I took cigarettes, lighter and a little folding cash and headed for the exit.

There was a pair of maggots festooned with enough Japanese hi-tech to up the UK balance of payments deficit by several thousand nicker hanging outside the house and they came to parade ready as I opened the front door. They clicked a few off before they realised I wasn't one of the stars of the show. A third maggot with a miniature tape recorder came running up to me. I looked for his slime trail but he must have been wearing wellies.

'Are you on the staff?' he asked.

'No,' I said. 'I came to line up the satellite dish. They're having trouble getting MTV.' I swear he looked towards the roof. As I body-swerved round him, one of the photographers gave me a look of recognition. 'Is your name Sharman?' he asked as I passed him.

'No,' I said. 'Lord Lucan.'

'Don't mess around, mate. I recognise you.' And he started firing his camera into my face.

'Get that fucking thing away from me. I warn you,' I said.

'It's my job.'

'It's your poxy face too, pal,' I said. 'Want to keep it?'

He backed away but kept pressing the button on his motor drive. The geezer with the tape recorder got the message and came after me. He looked a bit bewildered but realised that something was up and started asking the smudger who I was.

'His name's Sharman,' the photographer said. 'He's a detective. His bird got blown up by some nutters last winter, you remember.'

That really pissed me off. 'And remember what happened to them,' I said.

The reporter stuck his tape machine under my nose. 'What's happening, Mr Sharman?'

I plucked the recorder out of his grasp and slung it into the road where a cab ran over it with a satisfying crunch. 'That's happening,' I said.

'Great.' The photographer changed cameras and fired off more shots.

I walked over and grabbed him by the shirt collar and twisted it hard to cut off his air supply. 'Fucking stop,' I said.

'All right, all right, mate,' he choked. 'Don't get physical. I'll stop.'

I gave up. The other geezer was snapping away and it was going to be too much trouble to chase him too. I couldn't take on the whole world. I pushed the first guy away and walked off. The reporter was holding the wreckage of his Toshiba. 'You'll pay for this,' he screeched.

'Send me the bill,' I said and walked off.

They didn't follow.

I walked east and turned past the Curzon cinema into Shepherd Market. I was at the pub by five to seven.

Endesleigh turned up at five to eight. I still could not believe that this guy was a detective inspector. 'Been waiting long?' he asked.

'Not long enough to make a career of it.'

'You look a bit pale.'

'It's the beer. Want one?'

'Don't mind if I do.'

I ordered him a cold Becks, which if it was like the ones I'd already drunk wouldn't be. I couldn't believe that in London, in the hottest summer for ten years, there seemed to be nowhere to get a cold bottle of beer.

'Are you sure you're old enough to drink?' I asked when it arrived.

'Be careful, Sharman. I have to take that shit at the factory, but not from you. I'm old enough to take you out of here and lock you up. Just remember that.'

'Sorry,' I said.

'This beer is warm,' said Endesleigh.

'Tell me something I don't know.'

'Is there any ice?'

'The machine's broken.'

'Dear, dear, dear.' He lit a Benson and Hedges. 'So what's the SP?'

'I had visitors last night.'

'Who?'

'A trio of gunslingers from down under.'

'Do what?'

'What I said.'

'When the place was full of my men?'

'Dead right.'

'They had a bloody nerve.'

'Exactly.'

'And what exactly did they want?'

I told him the whole story. The whole, whole story, leaving nothing out. He listened and changed from Becks to Black Label and smoked his Bensons until I'd finished. 'Well, that's very interesting. Do you think they're telling the truth?' he asked as we waited for fresh drinks.

'Who?'

'The gorgeous girls from Curzon Street?'

'It's weird,' I said, 'but yes I do. If they were lying, why hire me?'

'Why didn't you tell me all this before?'

'I wanted to keep something back for a big finish.'

'The big finish could be you, son,' he said. 'One way or another.'

I agreed, but didn't say so.

'So this bloke Lorimar has had the black on the Pike family for nearly twenty years?' he asked after a moment.

'On and off.'

'And now the cupboard, if not bare, is at least locked.'

'Temporarily.'

'Could be years.' He was silent for a minute or two and lit another cigarette. 'Tell me what else you know about these Australian jokers?'

'I've got no names, except Lorimar, and that's probably fake if he was scamming the hotel trade. Elizabeth Pike's private detectives in Australia couldn't turn him up but I could try and find out.'

'Do that, and I'll check Interpol. He might have a record under that name in Australia. We'll check Immigration and the airlines but, Christ, they might have been here for years.'

'I wouldn't waste your time,' I said. 'I bet they didn't leave much of a trail.'

'We've got to do something. There are some very senior officers getting extremely anxious about the outcome of this.'

'And of course you've got to wear kid gloves yourself.'

'Of course.'

'So, are you going to tell the big brass what I've told you?' I asked.

'I'm not going to tell anyone. Normally I'd take a couple of chaps into that house and lean on those two until they cracked.'

'Yeah,' I said. 'And they'd deny everything. And then bring in enough lawyers with enough paper to keep you filing for a year. These aren't a couple of old scrubbers from the Aylesbury Estate, you know.'

'I am aware of that,' he said. And not too happy about it, by the look on his face.

'I'll help you out.'

'Will you?'

'Why shouldn't I?'

'It's not your style.'

'Give a dog a bad name, eh?'

He pursed his lips. 'I took a look at your file today.' He held the tips of his forefinger and thumb as far apart as they would go. 'It's this thick.'

'Public enemy number one?'

'Not quite, but nearly. I also spoke to an old friend of yours.'

'Who?'

'Danny Fox.'

'How is he?'

'Good. He's thinking of going back into uniform.'

'Promotion?'

'That's it. Down in the sticks.'

'He'll be a chief constable before you know it.'

'I don't doubt it. He speaks well of you, off the record.'

'And on the record?'

'He doesn't want to know. He says you're just the sort of skeleton in his cupboard that'll stop him becoming a superintendent.'

I pulled a face.

'He said you could have been a good copper apart from one or two character deficiencies.'

'Like?'

'Like you couldn't take orders, like you have too smart a mouth for your own good, like you developed a taste for certain illegal substances and latterly sticky fingers.'

I pulled another, longer face. Danny Fox had always known me too well.

'He also said you've cleaned up your act apart from the odd lapse now and then, and that I could trust you, up to a point.'

'Damned by faint praise.'

'Well, you know Danny Fox.'

'I do indeed. So?'

'So I'll take a chance and trust you up to a point.'

'You might not be very popular.'

'I'll take the risk.'

'If anything goes wrong, about as popular as a slug in a sandwich.'

He shrugged.

'Thanks,' I said. 'I appreciate it.' I looked up at the ceiling and lit another cigarette.

'The trouble is, you don't exactly help yourself.'

'How?'

'You shouldn't carry a gun. It'll get you into some trouble.'

'Are you still holding that over me?'

'Not if you come good with these Aussies and I make the collar. I'll forgive and forget. I'll get you next time.'

'If there is a next time.'

'With people like you, Sharman, there's always a next time,

count on it.' He slid off his stool. 'Thanks for the drink. Keep in touch.' He left the pub and vanished into the night.

18

I finished my own drink and left the pub too. It was past ten and dark, but the temperature was still way up and the humidity was about eighty per cent. I could feel the moisture in the air like a hot towel opening my pores, and I imagined I could smell the sourness of my own sweat.

The narrow streets and alleys in the market were still packed with tourists and office workers who didn't want to go home. Working girls and a bunch of raggity-arsed despatch riders in leathers or fluorescent cycling gear were draped over their bikes, drinking pints like it was going to become unfashionable at midnight.

I walked back to Curzon Street trying to avoid being jostled. It was a dipper's dream and I didn't fancy having my pockets picked as I went. I also didn't want any damn drunk crashing into the cut on my side. There were a few dossers trying to get some kip in quiet doorways but both they and I knew that Curzon Street was a bad area for that sort of thing.

There were no reporters or photographers hanging around the front of the house. Obviously something more important had come up. I rang the doorbell and Constance answered. 'Good evening,' she said. 'Miss Catherine would like to see you the minute you get in.'

'I'm on my way up now.'

I went up in the lift and knocked on Catherine's door. She answered stinking of gin and wearing a peach-coloured ostrich feather and silk dressing gown that would have given a conservationist apoplexy and the worms full employment for a year. She'd managed to hide the bruise I'd given her with make-up, and her face was only slightly swollen.

'Pretty sexy,' I said. 'I hope it's not for my benefit.'

'Hardly,' she shot back. 'I'm glad you've bothered to show up. I thought you were my bodyguard. I'm all alone and need guarding.'

'The only thing that needs guarding around here is the key to the liquor cabinet.'

'Very funny. Where have you been?'

'I had other fish to fry,' I said. 'But I'm back on the case as from now.'

'I'm in your hands.'

'Not literally, I hope.'

'Not even metaphorically.'

'Right,' I said. 'Close the windows and put on the air-conditioning. I'll do the same in my rooms. Leave the connecting door unlocked and I'll see you in the morning. I doubt if we'll have visitors tonight, but it's best to be safe.'

'Aye, aye, sir.'

'Sleep tight,' I said and went to my room. I checked any possible hiding places and closed and locked all the windows and drew the curtains. As I did so I looked up and saw a few thin, high clouds scudding across the sky and being drawn across the face of the moon like chiffon scarves. I switched on the air and as I felt the first icy draughts I took a bottle of gin, tonic, ice and lemon from the fridge, and collected two glasses and made a stiff gin and tonic in one. I sat on the sofa in my sitting room, turned down the lights and turned on the TV. I found a comfortable position and lit a cigarette. The late night news had plenty on the Pikes. It made interesting viewing, particularly as I knew the truth, or at least part of it.

Catherine knocked on the connecting door about twenty minutes later. I didn't answer and she knocked again, then opened the door. I saw her body silhouetted through the thin material of her dressing gown as she stood in the doorway.

'Surprise, surprise,' I said. 'I saved you some ice.'

'It's not what you think.'

'It never is, sweetheart.'

'Don't call me sweetheart, you sound like a trick.'

'Pardon me, I'm sure.'

'I'm scared,' she said.

'I told you I don't think those guys will come back tonight. It's tomorrow we have to worry about.'

'I'm still scared.'

'And you want the protection of my manly body. Don't make me laugh. You can take care of yourself – you nearly killed me this afternoon.'

'I'm sorry about that.'

'And that's all it takes. "I'm sorry" and everything's all right. Why don't you go see Elizabeth?'

She shrugged. 'She's gone to bed. I don't think she wants to see me.'

'I don't think I do either.'

'Can't you ever say anything nice? You're just a bastard like all men.'

'Do you want me to apologise for what I am?'

'You should. You think I came in here to get laid. I only came for a bit of company.'

'Get a dog.'

'You fucking bastard.' If she'd turned on the waterworks then I would have told her to get lost, but she just looked me straight in the eye. 'That was a lousy thing to say.'

She was right. 'I'm sorry,' I said, and I was.

'I didn't come here to get laid,' she said. 'I've been laid enough, thank you. I've had enough fucks to last a lifetime. What do I need you for? Or any man? I've had enough men to know what they're good for. Not much I can tell you. Anyway, Nick, you're looking at damaged goods.' She posed in a mockery of provocation. She arched her spine and threw her head back, put one hand behind her head and caught her hair in a bunch, and licked her lips until they shone wetly in the half-light. I have to tell you she looked good. Too good to resist. 'Damaged goods, Mister Private Eye.' And then she did start to cry. A long mournful sound that raised the flesh on my back and made the short hairs on the back of my neck prickle.

I moved towards her but she waved me away and went into my bedroom. I didn't follow her. What she was going through had to be handled alone, or not at all. When she wanted company she'd let me know.

I sat down, lit a cigarette and took a whack at the gin. It tasted oily and sweet and cold and I emptied my glass. I looked at the door, but left her alone and made a fresh drink. She came back into the room after about twenty minutes.

'Drink?' I asked.

'I've had too many already.'

'One more won't make much difference then.'

'Okay, just a weak one.'

I mixed her a little gin and a lot of ice and tonic and gave her the glass. She took it in both hands and sat on the sofa.

'Sorry about all that,' she said, and leant back against me. 'Must we have the air-conditioning on in here?'

'No, not if you don't want it on.' I went to the unit and fiddled with the controls and opened the french windows. It began to get warmer immediately.

'That's better,' she said and patted the seat next to her. 'Come and sit down.'

And even though I knew what was going to happen, and even after all we'd said, I went. As I sat she put down her glass and turned towards me. She said nothing and I said nothing in reply. She moved towards me and I could feel her body heat. She came into my arms. She felt slightly damp under the silk dressing gown she was wearing. Her mouth fastened onto mine like a leech onto a fat vein and she chewed at my lips like someone getting the last slivers of meat from a chop bone.

Did I respond? Did I ever. I held onto her like a drowning man holding onto a lifebelt. My hands began to caress her and she obviously liked it because she pulled up the skirt of her dressing gown and lifted her leg over mine and jammed her thigh into my groin and kept it there. She was both soft and hard under the smooth silk and as I ran my fingers down her back and over the rich curves of her bottom, the material was smooth with no bump of underwear.

We went at each other like slaughterhouse dogs.

It was sex, pure and simple. No talk or thought of love, no talk or thought of anything much. Just dirty, sweaty sex. It was filth and we both got off on it.

She made my body hum, too. We hardly spoke at all. We just let our nerve ends do the talking and the only sounds were more animal than human.

The sofa was too small and I dragged her into the bedroom. It was freezing in there. I slapped off the air-conditioning and tore off her silken robe and threw her onto the bed. I crawled all over her, and she crawled all over me and there wasn't an inch of each other we didn't explore.

When we called half time, there was no slice of orange, just a shared cigarette and more gin which we cooled with the remains from the ice bucket. When I lit the Silk Cut my hands were wet. I dried them on the bed sheets which were wetter. She draped herself in her robe which stuck to her body like a second skin, damp and dirty in the faint light from the other room.

She leaned over me with the cigarette in her mouth. The robe fell away from her breasts which were as damp and dirty as the silk she wore.

'More,' she said. Not begging or any of that shit. Just stating a fact. I took the cigarette from between her lips and dropped it into my glass where it hissed in the dregs of the gin.

We were caught in the grip of a vicious spiral of downwardly mobile hedonism that might not end until we self-destructed on some far-flung reef of carnal pleasure and were washed up on a bleached beach of cut glass, but we went along with it like kids after candy.

More she wanted and more she got. And by the time we'd both had more, our bodies were sore and bruised from the friction and my bandage was wet with fresh blood.

There seemed to be nothing I could do that would quench her desire. I fucked her in every orifice, but there constantly seemed to be more hungry holes to fill. Finally I could take no more and I fell asleep on top of her as the dawn clambered through the windows.

When I woke up there was no trace of her except for the cigarette in the glass by the bedside and I wondered if I'd dreamt the whole thing.

19

I came to finally about nine. I hadn't slept so well in months. I lay in my sleazy bed and thought about the previous night. I didn't know how I felt. A bit like the cat that got the cream and a bit of a jerk.

I rolled out of bed eventually and hit the shower. I let scalding water pummel some life back into my tired body and then turned the temperature to cold and let that pummel some life back into my tired brain. I tried to keep my bandage dry but didn't totally succeed. I shaved and cleaned my teeth and got dressed, then went looking for a cup of coffee.

I went down to the breakfast room. It was deserted. I ate breakfast alone and not even a servant came to interrupt my solitude. I'd much rather have eaten in the mucky little café in Tulse Hill where I normally went. At least there was some company and you could borrow someone's paper.

I left the dishes on the table and went back to my room. As I walked through the door the phone rang. I looked at my watch. It was ten o'clock precisely. I picked up the receiver. 'Hello.'

Silence.

'Hello,' I said again.

'Mr Sharman, it's Vincent.' His voice sounded strange.

'Vincent, what do you want?'

'I need to see you.'

'Well, come and see me then.'

'I can't. I'm down in the garage, would you come down?'

'What's it all about?'

'I can't tell you on the phone, just come down.'

'All right, Vincent,' I said. 'If you insist.'

I took the lift down to the garage level and walked in. The Rolls stood there, gleaming, with the driver's door open. The garage telephone receiver was off the hook and it hung down the wall by its curly wire. The concrete bunker smelt of petrol and exhaust, polish and, way back, old dirt and cold decay.

'Vincent,' I called.

No answer. My voice echoed around the interior of the garage. I went over to the car. Vincent's cap was lying on the driver's seat. The keys were in the ignition and the ignition was switched on far enough to allow all the power options to operate, but the engine itself was off. I heard the hiss from the air-conditioning system and I killed the ignition. Silence.

'Vincent,' I called again. Again my voice bounced off the walls and dropped to the floor like a tennis ball with loads of bottom spin.

I stood for ten seconds, then I heard something from behind the wall that separated the garage from the rest of the cellars. I turned on my heel and walked towards the empty arch and looked into the dusty darkness.

Someone touched a switch and fluorescent tubes winked on. I scrunched my eyes up against the glare. Vincent was standing, spreadeagled, facing one wall with his hands against the concrete. His uniform was dirty and crumpled and his hair was mussed. A short, wide man with thinning black hair, wearing a lightweight, beige, two-piece suit and a slightly darker shirt buttoned to the collar, sans tie, was standing beside Vincent with a heavy automatic pistol fitted with a silencer stuck into the chauffeur's kidneys. Another, taller, man with ginger hair, a leather jacket and chinos was leaning against a metal tool cabinet next to the light switches. He was wearing black leather gloves and in his right hand held another pistol, similarly fitted with a silencer tube.

'G'day,' he said. Even if his accent hadn't been Australian, and the voice the same voice that had threatened to kill me in my room two nights before, I would have recognised the gun and gloves anywhere. 'I thought we told you to be out of here last night,' he said.

'Something came up.'

'You should have gone.'

'I know, I'm a fool to myself sometimes.'

'You can say that again.'

'The police are still around,' I said.

'You don't say. Mates of yours, are they?'

'Maybe.'

'Maybe, huh? Maybe's right, mate. Got any with you?'

He didn't wait for an answer, but pushed away from the cabinet, dusted down his sleeve and walked round me, keeping the gun trained on my middle. He looked back into the garage. I followed him with my eyes but didn't move a muscle.

'No, I thought not,' he said. 'You don't like the cops, do you? And they don't like you. We're here for our money, pal.'

'Why tell me? I don't hold the cheque book around here. I'm just on hire.'

'I don't suppose you do, and we know exactly where you fit in. But as you decided to stay, you're going to get the money for us.'

'I don't think so.'

'I do.'

'What would you say if I told you there wasn't that sort of money around?'

'I'd say you were telling me lies. So don't spoil my morning. It's been fun so far.'

'The money is just not available.'

He laughed and showed a set of perfectly capped teeth. 'The situation has changed. Have you spoken to Catherine Pike this morning?'

'No.'

'No, he says. And you won't, mate.'

I felt an itching premonition alone my spine. 'Have you hurt her?'

'No, she's in fine shape. A real good-looking woman. I wouldn't mind a go at her myself, but I know where she's been, don't I son?' His eyes slipped towards his mate and then back to me.

'You do,' said the wide man.

I wondered if he did. 'Does she know where you've been?'

'Very amusing, I like a man with a ready wit,' said the ginger man. 'But don't get carried away with it or I'll have to alter your clock.'

'We're not even introduced and you're already getting playful,' I said.

'We know who you are, that's what's important. Now just lean against the wall next to the other monkey there and we'll see if you've been down the store and picked up another of those little peashooters like the one we took off you the other night.'

'Not even a slingshot,' I said.

'Against the wall or I'll rearrange your bloody face.'

I did as I was told. He stashed his pistol under his jacket and gave me a thorough frisking. I tried not to flinch when his hands roughly touched the wound on my side. The wide man moved slightly so he could cover both Vincent and me with his gun.

'All right,' said the ginger man when he'd finished.

'I told you,' I said. 'But maybe touching men is your thing.'

'Shut it,' Ginger said, taking his pistol out again and casually swinging it between Vincent and me. 'Now, to get back to young Catherine. We've decided that the only way to get our money is if we've got some real bargaining power. So Mr Lorimar's taken her on a little trip. He's known her a long time and he's not as choosy as me.'

'You slag.'

'Naughty, naughty. Don't get personal, Sharman, or I'll hurt you.'

'Where has he taken her?'

'Wouldn't you like to know? But I think we'll keep that our little secret until you' – he pushed his gun into my face for emphasis – 'get us the cash in untraceable old notes. Then she'll be back safe and sound. Sound as a pound. Yeah, man?' His eyes slithered to his accomplice again.

'That's right,' said the wide man.

'Is he telling the truth?' I asked Vincent.

He looked sheepish but said nothing. I took it as an affirmative.

The ginger man put his fingers to his lips. 'I didn't say you two could have a convo about it. Take my word, Sharman, she's ours and ours she's going to stay. Now, no police, just one million pounds sterling and the whore is yours.'

'You're living in a fantasy,' I said. 'Who the hell am I supposed to get a million pounds from? Tell me that.'

'Don't be purposefully obtuse, son,' he said and gestured around the bare walls. 'Use your head. The family is dripping with loot. It's coming out of their ears. Tell Elizabeth to get her hands on some of it. If she doesn't, her sister is going to turn up floating in the Thames. Just do it. Take the message like a good boy. We'll talk to you tonight. Stay by the phone. We'll be off now. Don't bother to come with us, we'll see ourselves out.'

They backed out into the garage proper, guns in hands, and I heard their footsteps on the floor and the small garage door open and close.

20

I stuck my head around the corner of the wall. The garage was empty except for the huge Rolls-Royce. 'It's okay,' I said. 'They've gone.'

Vincent pushed himself away from the wall and dusted his hands together. He was shaking and his face was pale.

'Are you all right?' I asked.

'I am now. Christ, I was scared. I thought they were going to kill me.'

'Come and sit down.' We went to the car and he sat behind the wheel and I sat next to him on the passenger seat. I lit two cigarettes and handed him one. 'So what happened, Vincent?' I asked.

He composed himself and closed his eyes as he spoke. 'Miss Catherine gave me an early call,' he explained. 'She wanted me to drive her to Covent Garden. We got there just after nine, but the shop she wanted to go to wasn't open, it was too early. So she did some window shopping and as it still wasn't open she told me to drive her up to Camden. There's a dress shop up there she buys a lot of stuff from. I drove through the bottom of Mercer Street, by the theatre, and a Transit van cut us up and forced me to stop.

Those two men who were here jumped out of the back of the van, and the one with the ginger hair stuck a gun in my face.'

'What about the driver?'

'He stayed put, I never saw him.'

'Was your window open.'

'Yes.'

'Didn't you have the air-conditioning on?'

'Only in the back. I had the partition up. I like fresh air.'

'So what happened then?'

'I had the back doors locked. I always do in traffic. There's a switch by the steering column. That ginger bloke tried the door. He said he'd shoot me unless I opened it, then shoot the lock. There was nothing I could do, honest, so I opened the locks. Then the ginger bloke got in the back and he said something to Miss Catherine that I couldn't hear because of the partition. Then the bastard hit her ... ' Vincent put his head into his hands.

'All right, Vincent,' I said. 'Take it easy.'

'Like I said, he hit her,' he went on. 'And then he pulled her out of the car, dragged her over to the van and pushed her into the back and slammed the doors. The fat bloke kept his gun on me. I couldn't do a thing. Then those two got in the Rolls. The ginger one was up front where you're sitting and the other in the back. Honest, Mr Sharman, I couldn't do a thing to stop them, I swear.'

'Okay,' I said. 'It wasn't your fault. Did you get the number of the van?'

'No, there was a piece of cloth over the plate.'

'Was it a plain van?'

He nodded.

'Colour?'

'Dark blue.'

'Fine, that's about half the Transit vans in London. And no one in the street did anything?'

'No, that street is quiet, there was no one about. And it all happened so quickly.'

I opened the ashtray on the dashboard and stubbed out the butt of my cigarette. 'Well, here we are.'

'Where?'

'In the shit.'

'I'm sorry,' he said and leant his head forward onto the steering wheel.

'I'd better go and tell Elizabeth.'

'God, she'll kill me.'

'Don't worry,' I said. 'I'll make it right. And for now, don't tell anyone about Catherine being snatched. Not the servants or the family, and certainly not the police, understand?'

He nodded. I left him sitting in the car, still shaking slightly and gazing through the windscreen at the blank wall opposite.

21

I went upstairs to Elizabeth's apartment. She was in her sitting room. There was a breakfast tray on the table.

'We've got problems,' I said.

'Tell me something new.'

'I'm serious.'

'What then?'

'I'll give it to you straight,' I said. 'Catherine's been kidnapped.'

'What?' she cried, and got to her feet, her face ashen.

'Kidnapped.'

'Are you sure?'

'Never more so.'

'But who would do such a thing?'

'Who do you think? The little firm that dropped by to see me the other night after killing Leee. Who else? They were serious when they told me they wanted their money.'

'When did it happen?'

'Just after nine this morning.'

'Where from?'

'The Rolls.'

'Where was the Rolls?'

'In the street, in Covent Garden.'

'What the hell was Catherine doing in Covent Garden at that hour? She didn't tell me she was going out.'

'She was shopping.'

'Was she alone? Where was Vincent while all this was happening?'

'In the car too.'

'Didn't he put up a fight?'

I shook my head.

'Is he here now?'

'Yes, downstairs in the garage.'

'You mean he just let her get abducted and then calmly drove back here?'

'No, he had two guns pointed at him at the time.'

'Did anyone in the street see what was going on or try and stop them?'

'Apparently not. You can do a lot on the streets of London these days before anyone calls foul.'

'Have you told anyone else?'

'Not yet, the kidnappers told me not to.'

'You've spoken to them?' she said in surprise. 'Did they telephone?'

'Better than that, I've seen them.'

'What? Are you serious?'

'I already told you, never more so.'

'When did you see them?'

'They just left.'

'They were here?'

'Yes, downstairs in the garage. They made Vincent bring them back in the limo, at gunpoint.'

'I don't believe this. You mean you spoke to them and you did nothing? Did you offer them lunch? The place is crawling with police and two men with guns drive into my house like they've been invited! Where's Vincent? I'm going to fire that incompetent fool.'

'Calm down,' I said. 'Losing it isn't going to help, nor is firing Vincent. And the place is hardly crawling with police. I don't think there's any here at all this morning. Even the news people have gone to pastures new.'

'I'm not "losing it" as you put it,' she said haughtily. 'And by the way, where were you when Catherine was abducted? Correct me if I'm wrong, but weren't you hired as a bodyguard?'

I was hoping she wouldn't ask that. If I hadn't been awake half the night, breaking the first rule of the game, screwing the client, I might have been with her when she'd been snatched. I went on the offensive.

'You're wrong,' I said. 'I was hired for all sorts of little jobs and all sorts of reasons. I inherited the job of bodyguard. I told you yesterday I wanted to go to the police, but you two talked me out of it.' I declined to tell her I'd already done just that. I was beginning to get pissed off again, at everyone connected with this little caper. 'Catherine went shopping early. She didn't wake me or else I would have tagged along. I can't be everywhere at once.'

'So what do these bastards want?'

'One million. The original price.'

'When do they want it? I haven't got that sort of money lying around.'

'Soon. They're going to contact me.'

'Why you?'

I shrugged. 'Why not?' But I was beginning to ask myself the same question.

'So what should I do?'

'About the money, nothing at the moment. Let me tell the police. This whole thing is getting out of hand.'

'No.'

'You're crazy.'

'Why?'

'Because it's not good policy to pay kidnappers. Catherine may be dead already.'

'Do you think so?'

'I don't know, but paying up won't guarantee anything.'

'So what should I do?'

'I've told you. Do nothing and I'll go to the police.'

'No. I'll pay. I'll get the money.'

I sighed. 'Where from?'

'From the business. We'll liquidate funds.'

'As I understand it, you don't have the authority.'

'I'll get it.'

'From?'

'From the board. David is the MD.'

'If you're determined to pay, I'm afraid you won't be able to go to the board.'

'Why not?'

'Because a thing like this has to be kept totally secret. Anyway, he may not agree.'

'She's his sister, for God's sake.'

'Half-sister,' I reminded her. 'A half-sister he accepted on sufferance and who is now turning out to be very inconvenient to have around. It might be better for the lot of you if she was dead. At least that would allow the will to go through probate.'

'Don't say that.'

'It's true. And as far as I can see, relations between you and him are a little strained too.'

'Not that strained. I'll speak to him now. Is he here?'

'I don't know. I told you, I haven't seen anyone this morning.'

'Except a pair of crooks.'

'Except a pair of crooks,' I agreed,

'Get out now, will you?' she said. 'I have to think.'

I couldn't blame her for being miffed, so I went.

22

I sat in my own apartment like a naughty boy being sent to bed early. I didn't like it, believe me. I sulked and smoked a cigarette and drank a beer from the ice box. An hour later the internal telephone rang. It was David Pike. He'd obviously been tracked down wherever he'd been and dragged home. He sounded well pissed off. 'Will you come to the morning room?' he asked.

'Of course,' I said and hung up. I put on a jacket and went downstairs. David and Elizabeth were waiting for me. The atmosphere in the room was so thick you almost needed a blow torch to get in. Elizabeth looked as raw as a bitten nail. David was as dapper as ever. He was standing by the window, done up to the nines in a charcoal grey double-breasted suit that fitted so well I suspected the hand of divinity in the tailoring. The look he gave me made me feel about as welcome as broken glass in baby food.

'What's all this nonsense I've been hearing?' he snapped as soon as I had closed the door behind me.

'I don't know,' I replied. 'What particular nonsense are you referring to?'

'You know very well,' he said. 'My sister, where is she?'

'Your guess is as good as mine. She's not here, is she?' He was beginning to get right up my nose and I wasn't about to be helpful.

'Stop it, both of you,' interrupted Elizabeth with a voice that was only a hair's breadth away from cracking up. 'It's Catherine you're talking about. She's been kidnapped and all you're interested in is scoring points off each other.' She was more on top of the situation than I'd thought she'd be, and perfectly correct.

'Okay,' I said and told David what Vincent had told me, and the kidnappers' demands. He looked at me all the time I was speaking, then went to the telephone and summoned Vincent. The chauffeur came into the room looking like he'd lost a tenner and found something nasty. He told his story too. And while he was talking, I smoked a cigarette and watched the smoke hover in the corners of the room like the ghosts of good intentions.

When Vincent had finished, David dismissed him perfunctorily and got back to me and Elizabeth. 'Who are these people?' he asked.

Elizabeth looked at me, then down to the floor and finally straight at David. 'They're people Catherine knows.'

'People she knows?'

'People from her past.'

'Christ,' he said. 'But why kidnap her?'

'Money. That's what it always is with us, money.'

He didn't argue. 'She brought them here.'

'They followed her.'

'Why?'

'They say she owes them money.'

'What for?'

'Blackmail.'

'Over what?'

'I can't tell you.'

'Then I can't pay.'

'Tell him,' I said.

So she did. The whole story again and I smoked another cigarette as she did so.

At the conclusion of the story David slammed a clenched fist into an open palm and Elizabeth jumped, and so did I a bit.

'I'm going to the police,' he said.

'No,' said Elizabeth. 'Get the money and pay.'

'Are you serious? I don't have access to that sort of cash.'

'Get access then. She's your sister.'

For a moment I thought he was going to refuse. They stared at each other until I thought the air would crack with the vehemence in their gaze. Finally David dropped his eyes. 'And if I can?'

'Then Mr Sharman waits for those men to contact him and he takes the money to them and gets Catherine back.'

'You mean you intend to let him walk out of here with a suitcase containing one million pounds in cash. The man's no better than a crook himself.' He didn't look at me as he spoke.

I didn't say anything.

'He's perfect, then,' said Elizabeth. 'At least he's got a chance of getting her back.'

'I don't believe I'm hearing this, Elizabeth,' he went on as if she hadn't spoken. 'Since Catherine came into this family's life there's been nothing but trouble.'

It was Elizabeth's turn to ignore his remark. 'The money goes with Mr Sharman,' she said.

'And we don't tell the police?' said David.

'That's what the kidnappers want.'

'I'm sure they do.' He almost choked.

'If it's any consolation,' I said, 'I told Miss Pike not to pay, but she wouldn't listen.'

'I just bet you did,' said David. 'How do we know you're not involved in all this? Why do they only communicate through you?'

'I'm not a thief, Mr Pike, or a kidnapper. It's not my game,' I said. 'And I resent the implications of that remark.' Blimey, I was starting to sound like a brief. 'I don't know why they communicate only through me.' Although I had a shrewd idea that they were doing it because they thought I was as bent as David Pike thought I was, and in so bad with the law that I wouldn't share anything with them. 'I'm happy to leave the whole thing to you. I don't think you should pay because once you've paid, you may pay again and again. I think you should go to the police with what we have and let them take over. They have the resources.'

'No,' interrupted Elizabeth. 'The police will screw it up and Catherine may die.'

'She may die anyway,' I said.

David went back to the telephone. He tapped out a number and waited while the connection was made. 'David Pike,' he said into the mouthpiece. 'I want a million pounds by close of business today. I want it in used fifty-pound notes, no consecutive numbers. I want it packed into a suitcase and I want it delivered here under armed guard. I want the guard to stay with it until further notice.' He paused. 'I don't know for how long. Get the security firm to lay on shifts of men.' He paused again. 'Don't bother me with details,' he barked. 'Just do it.' And he slammed down the phone so hard I half expected the plastic to split. He looked at Elizabeth. 'I hope you're satisfied,' he said and walked out of the room.

23

I looked at Elizabeth and she looked at me. 'You're in business,' I said.

'The money's not here yet.'

'It will be. And now I'm going upstairs. I need some time to think. See you later.'

I walked out of the morning room and took the lift. The house was quiet apart from the constant hum of the traffic from outside. I closed and locked my door behind me, lit a cigarette and went and sat next to the telephone. I called Endesleigh. He was at his desk. 'Fancy a drink?' I asked.

'I'm busy.'

'You'll be busier.'

'Why?'

'Something heavy is about to go down.'

'When?'

'Soon, maybe tonight.'

'Where?'

'Here, where else?'

He hesitated. 'Can you give me an hour? I'm tied up now. How about lunch?'

'An hour's okay. Where?'

'You can get a decent steak and kidney pudding at The Sun in Dover Street.'

'This weather?'

'Any weather.'

'I'll stick to the seafood salad,' I said.

'Seafood's for wimps.'

'So they tell me. What time?'

'Twelve thirty. Then we can be sure of a seat.'

'See you then,' I said and broke the connection.

He was waiting in the basement bar next to the restaurant when I arrived. The newshounds had indeed gone from Curzon Street. If they had known what I knew they would have been round in droves.

Endesleigh ordered me a beer. I had draught because at least I knew it would be cold. 'I've got a table,' he said and took me through to the restaurant. We were put in a corner where it was quiet. I studied the menu. 'Christ, what am I doing?'

'What's up?'

'Catherine Pike has been kidnapped and I'm debating between prawn and scampi.'

Endesleigh looked sharply at me. 'Come again?'

'Catherine Pike was snatched this morning from the back of that big Rolls limo. The kidnappers want a million quid. They've chosen me as their liaison in the house.'

'If you're kidding me ...'

'No jokes,' I said.

'When did this happen?'

'Nine, or thereabouts.'

'Who took her?'

'The Aussies who visited me the night before last.'

'Terrific,' he said. After a moment he continued, 'Have you found out anything about these mysterious Australians? Like the other two's names, for instance?'

'No,' I said. 'How about you?'

'Not a thing. As you said, they didn't leave a trail.' He sipped his drink. 'Why has no one informed us about Catherine Pike's kidnap?'

'I believe I just did.'

'Formally, not over fucking lunch, Sharman.'

'You're not going to be told formally. Elizabeth Pike is taking care of it. The money is being gathered together now.'

'I didn't think she had that sort of cash.'

'She doesn't. David Pike organised it. He's going to pay.'

'Like hell he is.'

'That's the way they want it.'

'It's not the way I want it.'

'And I work for them. If they knew that I was talking to you, I'd be out on my ear. Then you'd have no one on the inside. Calm down and listen. If we work this right, we can both get what we want.'

'Which is?'

'I want Catherine Pike back safe and sound. You'll get the kidnappers and the people who killed Leee the other night.'

'Tell me more.'

'I will, give me time. But first I want to be sure you don't go charging in this afternoon with all guns blazing. They've got someone in the house who passes on all the news.'

'Who?'

'I'm not sure.'

'Terrific. When do you do the swap?'

I shrugged. 'Don't know yet. They're calling me tonight to check the cash has arrived. They'll tell me then.'

'I could put a trace on the line.'

'And that'll blow everything and Catherine will be further up shit street than she is now. Besides, they'll probably use a portable. These boys aren't exactly green.'

'Christ,' he said. 'This could be more than my job's worth, you know that. And if it all goes wrong, you still come up smelling of roses.'

Roses always made me think of bad things but I didn't mention it. 'Hardly,' I said. 'It's not something I contemplate being easy to live with.'

'My heart bleeds,' he said sarcastically.

'But I am sure that if you go dancing into that house, Catherine Pike will die,' I said. And my blood went colder than the ice where the seafood was nestling, waiting to be laid out like the little corpses they were on a plate of salad. 'It's up to you, Inspector,' I said. 'It's her life in your hands.'

'So what do you suggest?'

'I suggest we wait until the contact is made. No one knows that I'm collaborating with you. Exactly the opposite in fact. I fix up the meet with the Australians and you wait with your blue-bereted friends. When I turn up, we close the net on this little firm once and for all.'

'I hope you're right,' he said.

'Not as much as I do.'

We ordered lunch, although I wasn't hungry, and went round the track a few more times and finally Endesleigh agreed against his better judgement to go along with my idea. There was only one condition. When the kidnappers phoned, I had to speak to Catherine before I agreed to anything. If she wasn't with them, they had to phone back when she was. Endesleigh insisted. If I had any doubts that she was alive, he was going to go into Curzon Street mob-handed whether I liked it or not.

I left the pub about three. I was sober but dying for a drink and my stomach was jumping like the prawns I'd eaten had been resurrected in my gullet and were doing a quickstep in my guts.

24

I went straight back to the house. Miranda let me in and seemed pleased to see me. I was pleased to see her too. 'Is Miss Elizabeth in?' I asked.

'In her apartment, with Mr David,' she replied.

I took the lift again and went and knocked on Elizabeth's door. She opened it. She was dressed all in blue. 'Can I come in?' I asked.

'Of course.' She stepped away from the door into the room, and I went in after her and closed the door behind me. David was pacing the floor like an expectant father on slimming pills. 'Where have you been?' Elizabeth asked.

'Around and about.'

'What would have happened if those men had phoned?'

'They're phoning tonight. I told you that. Have you got the money?'

'By close of business, no. But most of it will be here this evening. That's the best I can do,' said David.

'What do you mean, most of it?'

'Do you know how difficult it is to raise that sort of cash at short notice?'

'No,' I replied. I often find it difficult enough to raise the cash for a round of drinks at my local, but I wasn't about to tell him that.

'It's bloody difficult,' he went on. 'I've had to borrow most of it at a very high rate of interest until I can liquidate some assets.'

'It is family,' I said.

'Bugger the family. As if it wasn't inconvenient enough that Father died when he did.'

'It must be a real drag. How much are you short?'

'Right now, about two hundred K. The balance is coming in from a foreign subsidiary overnight. It should be here by six tomorrow morning, no later. If this gets out, our shares are going to suffer. Christ knows what the City would think.'

Dear, dear, I thought. If it wasn't one thing, it was another affecting the prices of his bloody shares. 'It certainly is a sobering thought.'

'Shut up for God's sake, Sharman, you're not helping.'

'I could care less, but it would be difficult,' I said. 'So I tell these jokers when they phone that I can deliver in full tomorrow, after six.'

He nodded.

'Right,' I said. 'I'm going to my room to wait for the call. I'll talk to you all later.'

Back in my room I kicked off my shoes, sat down and waited for the telephone to ring. I had a long wait. There was only one interruption. David came up at about seven and told me that the bulk of the money had arrived and had been stored in the safe in the study under armed guard.

It was after nine and I'd sent down for some food before the call came. 'Sharman,' said the distinctive voice of the ginger-haired Australian. 'Got the cash?'

'Not all of it.'

'If you're fucking us around ...'

'Take it easy,' I interrupted. 'Eight hundred thousand came in earlier this evening. The balance will arrive in the morning.'

'What time?'

'Before six.'

'You'd better be right. I'll phone you tomorrow at six. I'll give you your instructions then.'

'I need to speak to Catherine.'

'No.'

'Then no deal. I don't bring you any money until I know she's all right. I want to speak to her now and when you call tomorrow.'

I heard the silence grow long down the phone. 'Okay,' he said finally. 'But make it quick.'

There was another longer silence punctuated only by some muffled noises like doors opening and footsteps. Then I heard Catherine's voice, cracked and trembling, but unmistakably her.

'Nick, help me,' she said.

'I will,' I replied. 'How are you?'

'All right. Dry, they gagged me … ' And she was gone.

'Satisfied?' asked the ginger man.

'You fucker,' I said and the phone went dead in my hand.

I found Elizabeth and told her the news. 'Thank God,' was all she said.

I went back to my apartment and called Endesleigh at his office. 'It's on,' I told him. 'All the cash will be here tomorrow by six am. The Aussies are going to call me then with instructions.'

'Catherine Pike?' he asked.

'I spoke to her.'

'And?'

'She's alive. She doesn't sound too bad under the circumstances. She's shocked and scared and they've got her gagged, so I suppose she's trussed up too. I just hope she can get through the night okay.'

'Me too. I'm getting everything arranged at this end. I'll sleep at the station. Get back to me the minute they phone. And whatever the arrangements are, whether it's a meet a hundred miles away or in Shepherd Market, I'll have to have time to get my men organised. You'll have to use delaying tactics without being too obvious. I'm going to assume they'll lead you a bit of a dance. It depends how paranoid they are and how much TV they watch. They might not even tell you the full arrangements on the first call. It's possible they'll send you to a public phone. One thing, I can't see them coming close to where you are, it's too risky. They'll have to consider the chance that you've blown the whistle, but there's enough of the sods to keep you running around all morning and keep an eye on you to make sure you're alone. Anyway, whatever happens, if it's humanly possible I want my blokes in front of you, not following. I'll have a couple of car loads up here out of the way. You say the money will be ready by six. I'll have my men here at four. Now listen, Sharman, no blind drops. You have to meet them face to face and hand over the money in exchange for Catherine, or no deal, right?'

'Right,' I said.

'And make sure you speak to her in the morning.'

'I've told them that already.'

'You know I don't like this, don't you?'

'I know, but it'll work.'

'It better,' he said and hung up. I uncrossed my fingers and hung up too.

25

I was too wired to sleep. I put my shoes back on and wandered about my sitting room, then tried the connecting door to Catherine's apartment. It was still unlocked. I went through and stood in the empty sitting room and lit a cigarette. I opened the top drawer in the small bureau next to the french windows and poked around inside. I found her passport, Australian, in the name of Catherine Bennett. I turned to the page that bore her photograph and looked for a long time into the eyes that stared sightlessly back at mine, and hoped I wouldn't let her down when morning came. I put the passport back and closed the drawer.

I left the room by the door into the corridor and went back downstairs to Elizabeth's rooms. I knocked once and she opened the door as if she had been waiting for me.

'I'm sorry to bother you again. I'm getting a bit edgy up there on my own,' I said.

'It's no bother. I was getting a bit edgy myself.'

We both smiled, but hers looked, and mine felt, a little strained. 'Drink?' she asked.

'A small one.'

She went to the sideboard and poured me a brandy. I sipped at the drink. 'Can I look at the papers that Catherine brought with her from Australia?'

'Why?'

'Why not?'

She shrugged. 'All right. They're in Daddy's study. In the safe with the money.'

She took me down to the first floor and along the corridor and stopped outside a huge oak door with a brass handle. 'I haven't been in here since he died,' she said.

'I'm sorry if it upsets you.'

'Don't worry, I'm used to being upset by now.' She opened the door.

It was a large room, the same size as the dining room which I realised was directly below us. The room was decorated like a gentlemen's club, when gentlemen's clubs were only open to gentlemen, had names like 'Boodles' and old retainers crept around with bottles of whisky and syphons of soda water on silver salvers. The colour effect was dark brown and maroon. Dark brown leather chairs, shiny and comfortable looking. Dark brown wooden panelling, and bookshelves whose surfaces had a patina that only age and a great deal of polish could attain. Dark brown carpet and curtains. There was a quantity of maroon, leatherbound volumes on the shelves. I wondered if they had been purchased by the yard. Faded hunting prints hung on the walls. The ceiling was brown too, stained by nicotine and time.

A comfortable room indirectly lit by concealed bulbs of low wattage. A comfortable room where a man could escape from the pressures of family and business. A room where he could finally take a pistol and blow his brains all over the dark brown panelling. I noticed that a section of carpet behind the leather-covered desk that dominated the room was a slightly lighter shade than the rest. I guessed that was the result of cleaning the human tissue off the pile of the dark brown Wilton.

David was standing in the centre of the room talking to a

heavyset individual whom I had never seen before. The stranger was wearing a dark grey suit, white shirt with a dark tie neatly knotted and heavy black shoes that almost constituted a uniform, and there was a bulge under his left arm. I guessed he was our pet armed guard.

'What are you doing here?' demanded David. 'Have the plans been changed?'

'No, we go as soon as the rest of the money arrives,' I said.

'Mr Sharman wants to see the papers that Catherine brought with her,' explained Elizabeth.

'Why?'

'Because they're there,' I said.

I could see his face redden even in the dimly lit room. He obviously wasn't used to the hired help talking back in front of other hired help. It was bad for the MD's image. 'I don't know if I can allow it,' he said. 'There's a lot of money in the safe.'

'Which I'm going to take out of here in a few hours' time anyway,' I said. 'I'm not interested in that now. I want to see the papers. I don't want to take anything out of this room. I'm hardly going to do a smash and grab in here with an armed man in the same room. If I wanted to steal your money, Mr Pike, I can do it tomorrow morning with your blessing.'

'I suppose so.' David took a key ring with two large keys attached out of his trouser pocket. He went across to one of the bookshelves and touched a hidden lever. A section of wall as big as a small garage door swung smoothly open. Behind the shelving was a safe door only slightly smaller than the piece of wall that had concealed it. The safe door was old-fashioned, all filigree work and ornate decoration that made it as much a work of art as somewhere to stash the family jewels. The words 'SAUL AND NEPHEW BIRMINGHAM 1936' were inscribed in gold, raised letters, two inches high, inside a stylised shield in the middle of the door. Red poppies with green leaves and stems and fleur-de-lys were picked out in enamel paint round the edges of the door.

It was beautiful in sort of an industrial way.

There were two locks in the door and David inserted the two keys on the ring, one after the other, turned them and pressed down and pulled on the metal handle. The door opened smoothly on its counterweights. The inside of the safe was large enough for a tall man to step inside and stand comfortably. Metal shelves lined the interior. There was a big, new glass-fibre suitcase pushed to the back of the safe. I imagined it held the money that had arrived so far.

He ignored the case and took down a battered cardboard file from one of the shelves and a large briefcase that was lying next to it. He left the safe door open and carried the file and the case over to the desk. He opened the briefcase and took out a thick scrapbook with a creased and faded cover printed with huge daisies in sixties style. It must once have been brightly coloured but was now faded with age and use.

'This is everything,' he said, and went back and closed and locked the safe.

'I'd like to go through them.'

'I'll leave you to it then.' He gave the keys to the guard and said, 'I'll leave you in charge. Lock everything away when Mr Sharman is finished.'

'Yes, sir.'

'I'll wish you all goodnight,' said David.

'Goodnight,' I said in reply.

Elizabeth echoed the sentiment but made no move to go. David hesitated, then left the room and slammed the door behind him.

'Do you mind if I stay?' Elizabeth said to me.

'No, but this might take a while.'

'I don't mind. Take your time.'

'Has anybody ever been through these thoroughly?'

'I don't know,' she said. 'I've glanced at them, maybe Daddy did.'

I pointed to the chair drawn up close to the desk and facing the room. 'Do you mind?'

'Not if you don't. Daddy was sitting there when he died.'

I looked at the section of panelling behind the desk and wondered if the bullet had gone straight through Sir Robert's head or bounced around inside his skull for a split second and stayed there. I suspected the former with a big-calibre gun like a Webley, but I didn't ask. I could see no trace of a bullet hole in the wall and all the panelling seemed to be of a similar age, but I guessed that the Pikes could afford the services of a decent chippie to do any renovation that was necessary.

I sat in Sir Robert's seat and lit the desk lamp that was in front of me. I pulled the scrapbook over and opened the cover. The book was about half full of clippings from various newspapers. There was no indication what papers they were from or the dates that they were published except where the scraps themselves included that information. The earliest with a date attached was a yellowed cutting from *The Australian* of 8 January 1965 concerning the birth of Elizabeth Pike in England. That must have been about when Catherine's mother started the book. The last was a slightly fresher piece of newsprint from the *International Herald Tribune*, dated 20 December 1981, and was filled with rumours of a takeover of Pike's by an American conglomerate. I estimated that there were maybe forty clippings in between. Forty in sixteen years. Not bad for someone who shunned publicity, and all from papers that were not from his native land.

I could still see the lonely child in the sterile hotel rooms perusing the papers she found or bought or stole and cutting out articles about the stranger who was the father she'd never known. It was a sad thought. The saddest thing of all was that on the pages between the clippings was a series of drawings, crudely executed in a childish style. Little square houses with chimneys puffing smoke and flowers in the garden. Little cars and trucks with PIKE written on the side. Little cats and dogs and women pushing prams. One drawing was of three matchstick figures. The tallest wore a top hat and smoked a pipe. The middle figure wore a skirt and carried a shopping basket, and the smallest held a balloon shaded in red ink. Underneath, in childish capitals, was written: DADY, MUMY AND ME. On another page was scrawled in thick crayon: I LOV MY DADY BUT HE DONT LOV ME. I thought of my own daughter living in another man's house and felt tears prickle behind my eyes.

I closed the scrapbook and pulled the file towards me. I hesitated for a second and then opened the box that held Catherine Pike's early life.

There was the steamship ticket that had taken her mother away to her exile. Catherine's birth certificate, with the father's details left blank. School records and reports which were indeed as sketchy as she had said. Medical records for both Catherine and her mother. Her mother's death certificate and details of where and when she had been buried. I took out each piece of paper, one by one, and read them carefully. One particular document that had been folded and pushed down to the bottom of a doctor's file made me stop and think. I carefully smoothed it out and left it to one side. It took me more than an hour and a half to empty the file, and I had forgotten that the guard and Elizabeth were still in the room. When I picked up the pile of documents and put them back in the file she said, 'You were very thorough.'

'I'm sorry,' I said, looking at my watch. 'I quite lost track of time.'

'You must have been a good policeman.'

'Not really.'

'I'm sure you were.'

'Thank you.'

'Are you any the wiser?' she asked.

I smiled. 'Maybe.' I picked up the single sheet I had laid aside. 'Do you mind if I hold on to this?'

'What is it?'

'Something and nothing.'

She shrugged. 'Of course you can.'

'Thanks,' I said, and folded the paper again and put it into my shirt pocket. I stood up and put the scrapbook back in the case and spoke to the guard who was sitting ramrod straight in a leather chair by the door. 'You can put this stuff away now,' I said. 'I'm all finished with it.'

'Yes, sir.' He locked up the papers again and pushed the section of bookcase back to hide the door.

'It's very late,' I said to Elizabeth. 'I think I'll try and get an hour or two's sleep before dawn.'

'I'll try, too, but I don't think I'll succeed.'

'Try anyway,' I said. 'I'll see you to your door.'

She smiled and took my arm. We wished the guard goodnight and left the study and all the bad memories it held. I walked her upstairs to her door where I left her and continued up to my own apartment, where I undressed and lay on top of the bed and tried to sleep. But as hard as I tried, my thoughts kept straying back to the lonely child in a succession of hotels in Australia and the miserable life she must have led, and I could feel a terrible anger beginning to boil up inside me.

26

At five twenty-five the next morning I was lying in bed looking at the light coming through a gap in the curtains in my bedroom. As I watched it change from blue to pearl to white, and the rectangle it formed on the wall move imperceptibly across the room, the internal telephone rang. I hoisted the receiver and stuck it under my chin. 'Yeah?' I said.

'The rest of the money is here,' said David Pike into my ear.

'Good,' I said, and put the receiver down.

I rolled out of bed and went to the bathroom. I took a piss, cleaned my teeth, had a lick and a promise of a wash and went back to the bedroom. I put on my watch. Five thirty-three. I pulled on a shirt and jeans and stuffed my feet into soft leather loafers. I picked up the piece of paper I had rescued from Catherine's box file the previous night and dropped it into my shirt pocket. I was ready.

I lit a cigarette and took a bottle of soda water from the fridge, knocked the cap off and swallowed half the contents in a gulp. I leant against the frame of the French window and waited for the Australians to call.

The external phone rang at six on the dot. I picked up the

receiver. 'Sharman?' said a voice. I recognised the ginger man's accent.

'Yeah.'

'You know who this is.'

'Yeah.'

'Got the money?'

'It's here.'

'Good.'

'Where's the meet?' I asked.

'Hammersmith. There's a building site just off the flyover. Shakespeare Grove. It's Saturday, there's no one about. We've made sure of that.' He gave me directions. 'Take the big Roller. That's the only car we want to see.'

'It will be,' I said. 'Get Catherine to the phone.'

'You're wasting time.'

'I want to hear her voice,' I insisted. 'And make sure she's there when I bring the money. It's strictly a COD transaction this morning. Please don't ask for credit as a refusal often offends.'

'You're in no position to haggle.'

'Wanna bet?' I said. 'Now get her to the phone.'

The receiver his end banged against something hard and I heard a muffled cry. It was a woman's voice.

'Catherine?'

'Please,' was all she said and the phone was snatched away.

'Now get the money and get going,' the ginger man said.

'Okay, I'm on my way,' I said and hung up.

I took Endesleigh's card from off the bedside table and picked up the receiver again. I even punched out the first two digits of his office number before I gently put the receiver back. I never was much of a team player.

I left the room for what I thought was probably the last time and walked down the two flights to the first floor. I hesitated on the landing on Elizabeth's floor but didn't go to her door. If we had anything to say, we could say it later, if I was still around. If not, then anything we said now was a waste of time. So I kept going.

I knocked on the library door at seven minutes past six precisely.

David Pike answered the door. He was dressed in a suede Levi jacket and blue jeans. On some people, yes; on him, no. The security man was standing by the open safe, the big glass-fibre suitcase beside him.

'They've called,' I said, 'and made the meet. Is that the money?' I nodded at the case.

'Yes,' replied David.

'Is it all there?'

'Of course.'

'Doesn't look like much.' By the look on his face, David was offended by my comment. I changed the subject. 'What are you carrying?' I asked the guard.

'What?'

'Your gun, what is it?'

He looked at David, who nodded at him to speak. 'A thirty-eight Taurus.'

'Give it to me.'

'Not a chance.'

'We're wasting time,' I said to David Pike.

'Give it to him,' he said to the guard.

'I can't do that, I don't even know him.'

'For Christ's sake, hand it over,' I said.

'Do as he says,' instructed David. 'I'll take full responsibility.'

Reluctantly the guard unbuttoned his coat and slid the revolver from its holster and gave it to me. The gun was nickel plated with a short barrel and a nice heft. I checked the cylinder. It was fully loaded with five thirty-eight special cartridges.

'Thanks,' I said. 'I'll get it back to you.' And I slid the gun into the waistband of my jeans and pulled the shirt tail out to hide it. The metal of the gun was cool on my skin and it dug into my hip uncomfortably.

'Got any spare ammunition?' I asked.

The guard scowled and pulled his jacket back. In five loops on the leather of his shoulder holster were five spare cartridges.

'I'll take those too.'

He squeezed them out and dropped them into the palm of my hand. I put them in the back pocket of my jeans.

'So where is this meeting then?' asked David.

'That's my little secret,' I said.

'You won't leave here with the money unless you tell me.'

'Suits me,' I said. 'I don't intend to.'

'What does that mean?'

'You'll see.'

I walked past the guard and hefted the case. It weighed a ton, but I supposed it would have to with all that cash inside. I picked it up and took it over to the desk and hoisted it on top. The guard looked at David, but he calmed him with a glance. I flicked the catches and they opened. I lifted up the lid and looked at one million pounds sterling in the flesh for the first time. It was quite a sight. I heaved the case up and emptied the money out. The neatly banded bundles skidded across the leather, some tumbled to the floor. I went to the bookcases and started pulling out maroon-bound volumes and putting them in the case.

'What the hell are you doing?' demanded David.

'I'm doing what your father should have done years ago. I'm going to get a little justice for your sister Catherine.'

I finished filling the case with books, closed the lid and snapped the catches closed. I swung the case off the desk and felt it for weight. It was pretty close to when it had been full of cash.

'But the money –'

'Fuck the money, David Pike, and fuck you too!'

'I've never heard such –'

'Shut your fucking mouth,' I said, 'or I'll punch your fucking lights from here to Christmas.' Mercifully he did. 'I need the Rolls,' I said. 'Can you speak to Vincent from here?'

'If he's in his room.'

'He will be, I guarantee, and expecting the call. Tell him to meet me in the garage with the keys. Just that. Not a word about anything else, understand?'

'I will not.'

I took the Taurus from under my belt and pointed it at his chest and hiked back the hammer. 'Do it, David,' I said. 'Or it's goodnight.'

'You wouldn't,' he said.

'Want to bet your life on it?'

He obviously didn't. He stepped over the money on the floor and opened the top lefthand drawer of the desk. There were two telephones inside. He lifted the receiver of one and spun the dial. It was answered immediately. 'Vincent,' he said, 'will you meet Mr Sharman in the garage with the keys to the car?' He paused, then replaced the receiver.

Gotcha! I thought.

'Right, in the safe,' I said. 'The pair of you.'

'We'll suffocate,' protested David.

'You'll be okay for a few minutes. I'll make sure someone comes up and lets you out. Go on.' I gestured with the gun and both men stepped into the safe. I slammed the door, turned one key and left the room. I shlapped the case downstairs to the kitchen, using the stairs. Miranda was by the stove.

'Hey,' I said, 'want to do me another favour?'

'Certainly,' she said. 'What is it?'

'In exactly five minutes from now run upstairs to the study and open the safe. The key's in the lock. David Pike will be eternally grateful.'

'Why?' she asked.

'Don't ask,' I said, 'just do it.'

'If you say so.'

'Is there any sticky tape around here?'

'What kind?'

'Any kind, as long as it's strong.'

'Try the first aid kit in the top drawer of the dresser.'

I went over to a handsome Welsh dresser and pulled open the drawer. Inside was a big white enamel box with a red cross on top. I lifted it out by its handle and opened it. Packed inside was everything useful in the event of a small domestic accident, including a large roll of flesh-coloured Elastoplast. I took the roll and stuffed it in the side pocket of my jeans. 'Bless you,' I said and I kissed her full on the lips. She tasted like the best thing I'd tasted for ages.

'Another thing, Miranda,' I said.

'After that, anything.'

'Pack my clothes and stuff for me. I don't think I'll be back here in a hurry.'

I left her looking confused as I dragged the suitcase down to the basement garage.

Vincent was waiting for me. He was holding a set of car keys in his fist. I humped the case over to the car and wrestled it onto the front passenger seat.

'You wanted these, Mr Sharman?'

'Yes, I want them,' I said, and took the keys from him in my left hand. 'Where is the switch you told me about that locks the passenger doors?'

He opened the driver's door and leant in and pointed to a small stalk that protruded from the steering column. 'That's it.'

'Can you still open the doors from inside?'

'Yes, they all work independently, just use the handle as normal. They can't be opened from the outside, that's all.'

'Thanks,' I said. He turned as if to leave. I slid the gun from the waistband of my jeans with my right hand.

'Hey, Vincent.'

'Yes?' He turned and I hit him with the barrel of the Taurus. He went down on one knee. I hit him again and he went all the way down. I tossed the gun onto the front seat of the car. I took him by one foot and dragged him across to some cold water pipes that ran up one wall. His head bumped gratifyingly on the concrete floor as we went. I undid his belt, tugged it out of the loops and used it to truss him to the pipes. I went back to the driver's seat of the Rolls-Royce. I stuck the key in the ignition lock. The car started with a purr and only the gentlest vibration betrayed the fact that the motor was running. I engaged drive, slipped the hand brake and the monster limo crept towards the ramp. I touched the pad on the dash-mounted electronic eye and the garage door began to open. I pushed my foot on the accelerator and the car bumped up the incline and out into the mews. I left the door open behind me. I guided the car over the cobbles and left into Curzon Street, left again into Park Lane, through the lights, around Hyde Park Corner and west along Knightsbridge in the direction of Hammersmith. The traffic was light and the heavy car was a joy to drive. As I got used to the big steering wheel and the light power-steering, I started really to put it around the roads. I drove across the west of town at speed. It was a beautiful day, already hot, but I didn't use the air-conditioning, just opened the driver's window and guided the car one-handed as I drove.

27

I slid the Rolls into the narrow street at the back of the Shakespeare Grove development at seven o'clock precisely by the clock on the dash. I slowed the car to a crawl. The street was empty of life, not even a stray car or dog. A few nondescript cars and vans were parked up by the kerb. On one side of the road loomed the window-less back of a block of LCC flats, on the other the high wooden fence that guarded the building site, bare but for a few fly-posted advertisements for pop singles and albums and concerts and some brutal spray-painted graffiti. At the end of the street two chainlink gates that led onto the site stood open. Heavy-duty dry clay tyre marks scarred the broken pavement.

I halted the car and took the gun from the waistband of my jeans and the roll of Elastoplast from my pocket. I tore three long strips off the roll and taped the gun under the dash, butt outward, just far enough in so that it was invisible from above. I was careful not to cover the trigger guard or any of the moving parts. Then I tripped the switch on the steering column and locked all the doors from the inside.

I turned the Rolls onto the site and followed the rutted track, which tried even the smooth suspension of the big car, deep into the construction. I passed piles of brick and sand, silent plant machinery large and small, buildings that were complete, almost complete and mere foundations, until the road ran out in the middle of a yellow dust bowl between two mini skyscrapers shrouded with green netted scaffolding. In the middle of the bowl was parked a grey Mercedes estate. Three men were standing beside it. Through the slightly tinted windscreen I could just make out a blonde head belonging to the rear seat passenger.

I let the Rolls drift to within fifteen feet of the reception committee. I stopped the car and let the engine die. The dust it had raised settled gently. It was so quiet on the site that I imagined I could hear the particles patter on the bodywork of the Rolls-Royce. I stayed put and looked the trio over. It was made up of Ginger, the wide man and another man, older with thick grey hair and a face lined from years in the Australian sun. Ginger and the wide man each held the inevitable Berettas with silencers attached. The older man was unarmed. Ginger was grinning, obviously enjoying the whole thing. 'G'day, bro,' he said. 'Don't just sit there. Get out of the car and join the party.'

I did as I was told and stood by the open door. The three men crossed the space between us.

'Mr Lorimar, I presume,' I said to the older man. 'I can't tell you how much I've been looking forward to meeting you properly.'

The older man said nothing.

'Shut up,' said Ginger, his good mood evaporating. 'Turn round and put your hands on top of the car.' I did as I was told again. 'Search him,' he ordered his companion. I glanced round. The wide man slid his gun under his jacket and, being careful not to step between me and the ginger man's pistol, came close enough to touch me. He frisked me thoroughly from shirt collar to shoes. 'He's clean,' he said. 'No gun, no wire.'

'Smart boy,' said the ginger man. 'Where's the cash?'

'In the case on the front seat,' I replied.

'Get it,' he said to the wide man who walked round the back of the car to the passenger door and tried the handle.

'It's locked,' he said. He sounded surprised.

'I'll get it.' Before anyone could stop me I slid into the driver's seat and flicked the switch on the steering column. The passenger door opened and the wide man lifted the case out and threw it onto the bonnet of the Rolls as if it weighed nothing at all. He flicked the catches and opened the case, and as Lorimar and the ginger man's eyes shifted over to him, I reached under the dash and ripped the Taurus from where I had taped it.

The wide man swore in surprise at the contents of the case and hurled it off the bonnet of the car, scattering the maroon-bound books onto the ground. I brought the gun up into sight, cocking it as I did so. In the silence that followed his expletive and the violence of his action, the sound of the hammer locking back was as loud as a curse in church, and three pairs of eyes turned back to me.

'Drop the gun,' I told Ginger. His face turned into a mask of anger, but he didn't speak, just let go of his Beretta and allowed it to fall with a thud onto the ground where it raised a small cloud of dust. I stepped out of the Rolls. I needed to hold on to the element of surprise to splinter the group. The way they were standing, I couldn't keep them covered properly. 'You, Fat Fuck,' I said, and shifted my eyes over to the wide man. 'Take your gun out, just use the tips of your fingers. Don't get smart, or I'll shoot you down like a dog.'

He looked disgusted, but did what he was told and dropped the gun.

'Kick it away,' I said. 'Right away.'

He did as he was told again and the gun spun twenty feet and hit some breeze blocks where it bounced into a clump of wild grass. I ripped the strands of tape from the Taurus. 'Lorimar, come here,' I said. He obeyed. I pushed back his jacket and ran my hands under his arms and around his waist. Nothing. I pushed him away. 'All of you move back towards your car,' I ordered. 'We're going to talk.'

'You stupid bastard,' said the ginger man. 'We know you had the money, why didn't you just bring it and do the deal? Now we'll have to kill you.'

'Shut up.' I turned to Lorimar. 'Did you kill her?' I asked.

'Who?'

'Catherine Bennett, Catherine Pike, whatever you call her.'

'She's in the car,' he said.

'Not her,' I said. 'I mean the real Catherine Bennett.'

Lorimar's face seemed to collapse in on itself.

'I don't know what you're talking about.'

'Get real, Lorimar,' I said. 'It was a good try, and it almost worked, but not quite.'

'How did you know?'

'I didn't for sure, not until I found this.' I took the piece of paper I had found in the file out of my shirt pocket with the fingers of my left hand. 'You were very thorough. Too thorough, if anything, but you missed this. I went through Catherine's papers last night. The papers she brought from Australia. After all the trouble you went to to supply her with all the right credentials, I don't think anyone had ever gone through them before, or else they might have seen that there were too many things missing for someone who kept their whole life in a box. There were no photographs in that file, none at all. Up until her passport was issued, she didn't have one photograph. Not one in twenty-one years. A girl who was supposed to have attended drama school. I couldn't believe it. Even when she told me she'd only gone for a couple of terms, I still couldn't believe it. And there were no dental records. She must have been to the dentist at some time. And nothing in her own handwriting, not after she was a child. But the clincher was this.' I held up the paper. 'It was in a medical folder, pushed right down. I almost didn't see it myself.'

'What is it?' asked Lorimar, and his voice sounded weary and thin as a reed.

'A bill from a private hospital in Melbourne. A bill for an operation on Catherine Bennett. Dated 1969 when she was fourteen. A bill for the removal of her appendix. Now I know these surgeons are good, but not that good. I slept with that woman the night before last.' And I remembered her sweet belly, covered with a sheen of sweat as she pushed it into my face to be kissed. Apart from the indentation of her navel, from the rib cage to the triangle of curly blonde hair between her legs, her body had been as flat and white and smooth as if the skin had been airbrushed. 'She's never had an appendectomy, not on this planet,' I said.

The ginger man looked at Lorimar. 'You stupid old fool. I don't know why I ever listened to you. You told me it would be easy. I might have known you'd fuck it up.' And he made as if to hit Lorimar.

'Stand still or I swear I'll kill you.' I said. 'I haven't forgotten what you did to Leee.'

'You won't kill me,' said the ginger man.

'Won't I? Why do you think she got Elizabeth to hire me?'

His eyes narrowed. 'Is that why you're here?'

'No,' I said. 'I don't think you understand why I'm here.' I thought again of the lonely child with her book of scraps. 'Let's just say I wanted to see your face when you realised that you weren't going to get any of the money.'

He spat on the ground, but said nothing.

'Did you kill her?' I asked Lorimar again.

'It was her own fault.' He was almost pleading. 'You don't understand. She wouldn't have anything to do with Pike. In the end she hated him as much as Joanna did. I told her she could have a good life with him in England, but she didn't want to know. She preferred hooking on the streets. That was where I found her again. She was diseased and strung out on speedballs, but she still wouldn't take the money he left for her.'

'You got her to change her mind.'

'I did,' said the ginger man, and looked well pleased with the memory.

'You're a fucking scumbag,' I said.

The ginger man smirked but said nothing. Scumbag was probably a compliment where he came from.

'You still haven't answered my question, Lorimar. I won't ask you again. Did you kill her?'

'She would have been dead anyway within a few months,' said Lorimar.

'So you did.' I suddenly felt very old.

'He helped her on her way,' said the ginger man. 'Let's put it that way.'

I did feel like killing all three of them, there and then, but I'd come that far and I wanted to know a little more. 'So who's that in there?' I nodded over at the Mercedes.

'A girl we knew,' said Lorimar.

'And what did you have on her?'

'She owed money. She was broke. She was glad to do it. She looked a lot like Catherine, same hair, same eyes. As for the photographs, you're right. Our girl just didn't have any, none that fitted in with being Catherine Bennett.' He looked first at me and then at the ginger man. 'How was I supposed to know he'd sleep with her?' The ginger man looked at Lorimar like death.

'So who is she?' I asked.

'Who cares?' said the ginger man. 'Just another cunt.'

'She called herself an actress,' said Lorimar. 'But she was lousy. I don't think she ever got a part.'

'She can't have been that bad,' I said. 'She took everyone in when she got here. You took a hell of a risk.'

'It was a hell of a prize,' said Lorimar.

My right hand was getting tired and cramped from holding the heavy pistol and I swapped it to my left. 'Did she know you'd killed the real Catherine?'

'What do you think?' asked Lorimar.

'And what about Robert Pike?' I asked. 'Did you help him on his way too?'

'I told him the truth about her, and threatened to make it public,' said Lorimar. 'I suppose he just couldn't face losing her twice. Or maybe he couldn't stand to be made a fool of.'

I remembered then what I had said about suicides to Elizabeth back in my office.

'But why? You had a good deal going.'

'She stopped paying us,' he said. 'In the end I think she really believed she was his daughter.'

'I am,' said Catherine.

In all the excitement no one had seen her get silently out of the Mercedes. In the bright daylight she looked a lot older and more worn than I remembered. Her dress was wrinkled and dirty and had sweat stains under the arms, and her bright hair had turned dull and brassy. She had lost a shoe and leant against the car for balance. 'You killed my daddy,' she said to Lorimar, and I saw the sun reflect off the object she held in both hands. Somewhere in the back of the car she had found a screwdriver. She tottered towards him, one high heel on, one off, and drove the shank of the tool two-handed up into his throat, up through his mouth and into his brain. Blood spurted from his nose and from between his lips and spattered down the front of her already ruined dress.

Lorimar clutched at the brightly coloured plastic handle that protruded from just above his adam's apple and tried to say something. But his voice was ruined and what emerged was something between a scream and a sigh. He lost his balance and fell back onto the ground. As he hit the yellow dust, it puffed up around him and settled on his body and the pool of red that pumped from his neck and soaked the earth.

I looked into Catherine's eyes and in that split second knew that since I had seen her last she had gone through the barrier that separates the mad from the sane, and I doubted if she could ever return.

The ginger man took his chance and dived for his gun. As if on cue, the wide man took off for the clump of weed where his had ended up. I snapped off a shot at the ginger man and missed by a mile – I could never shoot lefthanded. The echo from the shot rang round the building site, bouncing back off every surface until it sounded like a hundred shots. I tossed the gun back to my right and fired double action at him again, and missed again. He had his gun and rolled behind the protection of the Rolls's bonnet.

I fired at the wide man's back and saw a puff of dust flower on the back of his jacket, high up on the left side. But he kept running and slid down beside the breeze blocks and I knew I'd done little serious damage. The ginger man popped up from his cover and pulled the trigger of his Beretta. I felt as if someone had clobbered me on the side of my head with a baseball bat. I dropped to the ground and rolled behind what cover the empty suitcase provided and hugged the dirt like it was a long-lost lover I hadn't seen for years. I saw blood dripping from my head onto the ground and heard and felt two more bullets tear into the case as he fired at me again and again.

When I'd been hit I'd lost my gun, and I thought my time had come, when suddenly from behind me I heard a voice, amplified by a loud hailer, echo around the site. It seemed to come from behind me and to the right, but I couldn't be sure. 'Armed police, throw down your weapons,' the voice ordered. And right then I knew what a condemned man feels like as a last-minute reprieve arrives at the place of execution, when the black hood is on and the hangman is about to spring the trap door.

The wide man found his gun and stood and aimed it in the direction that the amplified voice had come from. He fired and the silenced pistol kicked in his grip with a sound like a muted hand clap. Louder shots came from behind me and the wide man stepped back with a look of surprise on his face, dropped his gun, folded to the ground, kicked his feet for a few moments and went very still. The ginger man leapt from behind the car and grabbed Catherine. Holding her in front of him as a shield, he walked backwards, dragging her as he went, past the Mercedes and towards one of the scaffold-covered buildings. As soon as he touched her, the police fire stopped.

I cleared my head with a shake that sprayed blood down my shirt and scrambled for the Taurus. Endesleigh came running round the back of the Rolls, gun in hand, closely followed by Sutherland. Endesleigh ducked down and threw me back against the side of the car. 'Shithead,' he said. 'What the fuck do you think you're playing at?'

I sat and looked at him in a bemused fashion. Maybe not bemused, maybe stupid. Meanwhile Sutherland ran over to Lorimar, took one look and shook his head. He crabbed across the dirt to the wide man, picked up his Beretta, stashed it in one of his many pockets and touched the wide man's throat. He came back to where Endesleigh and I were waiting. 'Both gone, guv,' he said.

'Call it in,' said Endesleigh. 'And make sure that ginger-headed bastard doesn't get away. With or without the woman, but particularly with.'

Sutherland nodded and loped off without a second glance at me.

'How did you know … ?' I asked at length.

'We had a man in Curzon Street all night. While I was waiting for you to call, he saw you drive away in this thing.' Endesleigh rapped on the side of the Rolls-Royce. 'And five minutes later I get a call from David Pike screaming blue bloody murder that you'd locked him in his own safe, stolen a gun and the car, beaten up his chauffeur, left the ransom money and pissed off God knows where. Why didn't you call me like we arranged?'

'I knew it was going to get heavy.'

'You put Catherine Pike's life in danger. Luckily our man followed you, and had the nous to get directly on to me.'

'She's not Catherine Pike,' I said. 'Catherine Pike is dead. She's been dead for years, poor cow. Lorimar, or one of his little firm, did for her when she wouldn't play ball and come over here and scam Sir Robert. They disposed of the body so it couldn't be identified and put in a ringer. Now she's flipped out. She killed Lorimar. She practised a little DIY on his vocal chords.'

Endesleigh looked over at Lorimar's body. 'Jesus.'

'That's why I clobbered Vincent. There was no kidnap. He delivered her on a plate.'

'You're bleeding,' said Endesleigh.

Tell me something I don't know, I thought. I put my hand gingerly to the side of my head and it came away red with fresh blood. 'I bet you passed all your observation tests at Scouts,' I said as dryly as I could. I stood up and leaned into the open door of the Rolls, opened the glove compartment and found a pack of tissues. I looked in the mirror and saw that the bullet from the ginger man's gun had nicked a quarter-inch piece out of my right ear lobe. I stuck a tissue to it to stem the flow and said to Endesleigh, 'We're wasting time.'

'We nothing. This is police business. You're hurt, and should be under arrest. You stay here.'

'Not on your life. Where you go, I go. I'm in on this until the finish.'

He thought about it for a second. 'Come on then,' he said. 'But if I get fired I hope you offer me a partnership.'

'Just say the word.'

He was off and running like a bloody racehorse and I had the greatest difficulty keeping up, although I wasn't going to let him know that. When we reached the building the ginger man was heading for when last seen, all I could see were black spots in front of my eyes, but I didn't disgrace myself by throwing up, although my breathing might have been a little on the ragged side.

'They're up there, guv,' said Sergeant Sutherland who made a pointed display of ignoring me, much to Endesleigh's amusement.

'Are you sure?' he asked.

'Sure. Johnno and Bill saw them go in and they haven't come out.'

'I'm going up,' said Endesleigh. 'Who else is here?'

'Nobody, thanks to him,' replied Sutherland, and I think he meant me. 'But there's more on the way.'

'Don't endanger the woman,' said Endesleigh. 'I don't want anyone taking pot shots if she's within five yards of the ginger bloke.'

'Do you want anyone to climb the scaffolding on the outside?'

Endesleigh thought about it. 'No,' he said. 'If there's too many of us up there, we'll end up shooting at each other. You lot stay down here and wait for the rest. Perhaps he'll come down of his own accord.'

'Fat chance,' said Sutherland.

'And don't make a move until you hear from me.'

'OK, guv.'

'I'm coming with you,' I said.

'I was afraid you'd say that. But I warn you, my first concern is the woman.'

'Mine too.'

We went inside the building. It was a shell with floor and stairways in place but little else. The scaffolding was up so that outside work could be done. Because of the safety netting around the scaffolding, the interior of the building was cool and dark and green like the inside of a fish tank. There were two sets of stairs leading up, one at the front and one at the back of the building. I took the back.

The stairs were wide and we climbed them in tandem. Each time we came to a floor, we both peered across the bare concrete looking for any sign of life. As soon as we were sure it was clear we gave the high sign and started climbing again. There were ten floors in all By the time we'd both reached the seventh floor I think we both realised that Ginger and Catherine were going to be on the roof.

When we got to the tenth floor we walked across to meet each other. There was only one way up to the roof itself, a narrow metal staircase just wide enough for one person to climb at a time. The stairs went right up to a hole in the roof. The hole was open to the sky. Ginger had chosen well.

'I'll go first,' I said.

'No, I will,' insisted Endesleigh. 'You're a member of the public. You know the old motto: "To protect and serve".'

'If you insist.'

He clambered up the metal stairs in front of me, poked his head through the hole and looked across the roof. A bullet spanged against the concrete by his head and he ducked back. 'He's over on the corner, using some machinery and stuff as cover. She's with him. We can wait him out. Stick our heads up every now and then. When he runs out of ammunition we'll have him.'

'We don't know how much ammunition he's got,' I said. 'He might save the last bullet for the woman. Is the scaffolding right up to the roof?'

'And a bit above.'

'So no snipers?'

'No, they'll never get a clear shot.'

'Helicopter?'

'A bit iffy,' he said. 'I'll have to go down a couple of floors and come up the outside.'

'I was hoping you'd say that.'

'You're not volunteering?'

'Can't stand heights. I'll stay here and attract his attention. He doesn't like me.'

'I'm amazed. Give me ten minutes.'

I looked at my watch. 'Okay.'

He went back down the metal stairs then down the wider

stairs towards the ninth floor and vanished from sight. I was dying for a cigarette but I'd lost them somewhere. I flipped out the cylinder of the Taurus, discarded the three empty cartridge cases and re-loaded with three of my spares. I stayed at the top of the stairs, keeping my head down. When the ten minutes were up, I risked a look through the hole in the roof. Ginger was looking straight at me. He was holding Catherine round the neck and using her and a cement mixer and some bags of cement as cover. He fired off two snap shots which came close enough for me to hear. I ducked back down and I could still see Catherine's face. She was as white as a sheet and her blue eyes seemed to be burning out of her skull. She was disintegrating in front of me. I felt that terrible anger burning my guts again. I stuck my head out again and Ginger fired, and as a counterpoint to the slap of his silenced pistol I heard the deeper bark of a police-issue Colt from below.

I ducked down and back up in time to see him turn and fire over the edge of the roof. He let go of Catherine and she turned and lashed out at him with her nails. He screamed as her fingers raked his face. The gun went off harmlessly in the air and the breech of the Beretta blew back. Catherine was still too close to him for me to risk a shot. He pushed her and she stepped back. She lost her footing on the edge of the roof and fought for balance, her arms cartwheeling.

I pushed through the hole in the roof and ran towards her. She stepped back into space and her fingers caught at some loose netting which tore away from the scaffold. As she fell I caught her arm. The weight of her pulled me down onto the roof and the Taurus flew out of my grip, went over the edge and clattered down the scaffolding. The unfinished concrete cut into my chest and I felt the wound on my side tear open. Catherine was swinging like a pendulum on the end of my wrist. She started hitting and ripping at me with her other hand. I looked down and there was at least forty feet of space before the first platform of planks. If it was the same all the way round, I was done for. Endesleigh couldn't possibly get up to the roof.

I looked into Catherine's face and saw the madness burning in her eyes as they looked up at me. I turned my head and saw Ginger, blood pouring from the scratches on his face and a terrible smile on his lips, take aim at me. He snarled when he realised he was out of ammunition. He ejected the empty magazine, pulled another from his pocket, slapped it home and worked the breech to chamber a round. He brought the gun up and drew a bead on my head. I hung on to Catherine even though I knew it was over. I was so scared, I was hollow, and I knew if I shook I'd rattle. I was too frightened even to close my eyes. They were riveted to the big black hole in the ugly, bulbous silencer screwed to the barrel of the Beretta. Then I noticed movement at the far side of the roof and Endesleigh's head and gun hand poked over the top of the roof. Thank Christ, I thought.

Endesleigh fired and the bullet hit Ginger just as he squeezed the trigger of the Beretta. I saw his face register surprise and the gun moved as he fired. I felt as if I'd been kicked in the leg, hard. Ginger swung round and fired at Endesleigh. Endesleigh fired again and the ginger man went down on one knee and fired back. A bullet hit him in the shoulder and knocked him half round, but he kept firing, the big gun shaking in his fist. Another bullet went through his neck and blood fountained. He aimed one last futile shot before he fell forward onto his face.

I stayed where I was and, believe me, the concrete I was lying on felt good enough to eat.

Catherine was still slashing at my hand and I felt as if every tendon and muscle in my arm was being ripped out, and my leg burned as if it was on fire. I was close to blacking out and I felt Catherine's hand slip through mine. I concentrated hard on holding her. Endesleigh clambered onto the roof, kicked the

Beretta far away and ran to me. He leant over the edge of the roof and reached down to take some of the strain of Catherine's weight. Together we pulled her back onto the roof.